PRAISE

DON STRACHEY NOVELS

"Lively, skillful…highly recommended."

The New York Times on *On the Other Hand, Death*

"As much travel memoir as mystery, this tenth in a series spanning three decades is supremely satisfying as both."

Bookmarks on *The 38 Million Dollar Smile*

"As always with the Strachey novels, the murder and mayhem takes a back seat to the keen social criticism and defiant wit of our detective."

Maureen Corrigan of NPR,
naming *Death Vows* one of the top five mysteries of 2008

"A gripping, fast-paced mystery."

Booklist, on *Strachey's Folly*

"A joyous ride…the novel is like a classic screwball comedy of the 1930s."

The Berkshire Eagle on *Cockeyed*

MLR Press Authors

Featuring a roll call of some of the best writers of gay erotica and mysteries today!

Derek Adams	M. Jules Aedin	Maura Anderson
Victor J. Banis	Jeanne Barrack	Laura Baumbach
Alex Beecroft	Sarah Black	Ally Blue
J.P. Bowie	Barry Brennessel	Michael Breyette
P.A. Brown	Brenda Bryce	Jade Buchanan
James Buchanan	Charlie Cochrane	Karenna Colcroft
Jamie Craig	Kirby Crow	Dick D.
Ethan Day	Diana DeRicci	Jason Edding
Angela Fiddler	Dakota Flint	S.J. Frost
Kimberly Gardner	Roland Graeme	Storm Grant
Amber Green	LB Gregg	Drewey Wayne Gunn
Kaje Harper	Jan Irving	David Juhren
Samantha Kane	Kiernan Kelly	M. King
Matthew Lang	J.L. Langley	Josh Lanyon
Clare London	William Maltese	Gary Martine
Z.A. Maxfield	Timothy McGivney	Lloyd A. Meeker
Patric Michael	AKM Miles	Reiko Morgan
Jet Mykles	William Neale	Willa Okati
L. Picaro	Neil S. Plakcy	Jordan Castillo Price
Luisa Prieto	Rick R. Reed	A.M. Riley
George Seaton	Jardonn Smith	Caro Soles
JoAnne Soper-Cook	Richard Stevenson	Liz Strange
Marshall Thornton	Lex Valentine	Haley Walsh
Missy Welsh	Stevie Woods	Lance Zarimba

Check out titles, both available and forthcoming, at
www.mlrpress.com

RED WHITE
BLACK AND BLUE

A Donald Strachey Mystery

RICHARD STEVENSON

mlrpress
www.mlrpress.com

Copyright 2011 by Richard Stevenson

Published by
MLR Press, LLC
3052 Gaines Waterport Rd.
Albion, NY 14411

Visit ManLoveRomance Press, LLC on the Internet:
www.mlrpress.com

Cover Art by Deana C. Jamroz
Editing by Judith David

Print format
ISBN# 978-1-60820-362-8
Also available in ebook format
ISBN#978-1-60820-363-5

Issued 2011

Two apologies:

One for reinventing recent New York State political history for my own purposes; another for inventing a Motel 6 in Troy, New York, whose TV channel selections include Turner Classic Movies. Never happened, never will.

My thanks to the organization Democrats in Bucks County, Pennsylvania, where Joe Wheaton and I volunteered on the Kerry and Obama presidential campaigns.

Thanks especially to Kathy and Allen, Richard and Elin.

This estimable gang is more ethical than the Dems in this novel, and a lot more fun.

CHAPTER ONE

"Don, my man! Thanks so much for coming in. I'd've shlepped out to your office on Central — Christ, that's how important I think this is — but as you can see it's already pre-election shock 'n' awe around here, and I'm lucky if I can drag my sorry ass out of this madhouse before the bar shuts down at Jack's at ten. What can Beryl get you? Coffee? Green tea? A Cinnibon from downstairs? You're not vegan, are you?"

Loosening his damp grip, Dunphy chuckled at his meant-to-be mot, and I seated myself on the office chair nearest his commodious desk, which was about as orderly as mine.

"Albany tap water would be fine. I walked over here, and it's warm for June."

"What, water that comes out of a pipe? That's novel. I'm not sure we have any of that. We do have about forty crates of water that comes out of plastic bottles that might or might not cause liver cancer. In fact, every time I see the senator swig from a bottle of Dasani at an event, I think, fuck, some nasty tumor he picked up from all the plastic shit we all drink out of is metastasizing at that very moment, and just about the time Shy is elected governor he's going to get a diagnosis that says he has about six weeks to live." Dunphy yelled toward his open office door, "Beryl, can you get Don some H2O?"

"Okay, commander," a strained voice came back.

"Beryl's eleven years old and has a master's in political science from NYU. I depend on her for everything. Politically, she knows where all the bodies are buried in the state of New York, and she's got it all on her laptop."

"Good for Beryl. But if she already knows where the bodies are buried, I'm not sure why you need me."

"We'll get to that," Dunphy said off-handedly as one of the multiethnic array of slender young women and men who sat punching things into laptops in the outer office trotted through the doorway with a foam cup and a bottle of Poland Spring water.

"Don here only drinks Albany tap water, but he'll just have to adjust down," Dunphy said as the young woman gave her boss a look.

"Shut the door, would you please, Beryl?"

Dunphy was as quick and alert as his young assistant, but his appearance wasn't nearly so fresh. In chinos, loafers, and a pale blue sports shirt, the director of State Senator Sylvester "Shy" McCloskey's gubernatorial campaign was one of those men who had probably looked fifty-five when he was twenty-five — paunchy, jowly, bright-eyed and cheerfully pink-faced — and would continue to appear to be about fifty-five until a heart attack killed him at seventy-one. The view out the ninth-floor window behind Dunphy looked up State Street at the New York State Capitol, gray and dungeonlike even in the late spring sunshine, a structure as inert on its foundations as its legislative inhabitants, now more than two months late, as usual, with the state budget.

"Before we go any further," Dunphy said, "I take it that you support the senator's candidacy for governor. The people who recommended you for this project said they assumed you would, but of course I have to ask. Otherwise, there's no point in our going on."

"Sure. I'll vote for McCloskey."

"You don't sound one hundred percent convinced."

"I don't agree with your guy on everything. He's too timid, I think, on getting redistricting out of the hands of the Legislature. And on public financing for campaigns he's as retrograde as everybody else. There are a couple of other things, too. But who else could I support? Louderbush is way out in right field, and in the general election it's likely to be Merle Ostwind. I'm trying to recall, but the last Republican I can think of who I might have voted for was Abraham Lincoln."

"Yeah, the other party peaked in 1865. It's a shame. A healthy democracy needs two parties both working for the common good. Not one dedicated to screwing the poor and the middle class and the other one busy screwing itself every chance it gets."

"And we get another chance to screw ourselves this fall."

"Ah, but that's where you come in, my friend." Dunphy forced a sour smile. "I'm sure you understand that if Assemblyman Louderbush wins the Democratic primary, we're all but fucked in November. The New York State electorate can be cranky, but it's not by and large clinically insane. Voters don't at all mind placing Republicans in the governor's mansion — even mediocrities like George Pataki — if our party comes across as too arrogant or too uppity-smarmy or too indictable. Or — and this is why I have invited you here today — if we offer voters candidates like Kenyon Louderbush, who's too weirdly out of step with the generally mild and centrist thinking of most of the state.

"All the polling confirms it; Louderbush has an electorally formidable primary following. They are mostly deranged Tea Partiers who think the New York State GOP is a secret agent in the employ of European state socialism, and these folks would rather have a right-wing Dem than a Nelson Rockefeller-style commie-Republican in office. So they're reregistering Democratic — switching from Republican or independent — to get Louderbush the nomination in September. Then he'll of course lose to mild-mannered Mrs. Ostwind, and it'll be four years of Pataki Lite.

"Which would be very lite indeed. The state will stagnate and our party will fall into disarray. Beelzebub will reign, in the form of more investment in prisons than in higher education, minimum-wage privatization of just about every civic function, and teachers being required to stay late and mow school lawns and shovel snow. Our generous friends the unions will have conniption fits. The Legislature, of course, will continue to lie on its back, its legs over its head, transfixed by its own butt hole. Within a period of just a few years, New York State will turn into Mississippi or Idaho or some such benighted bog — an international laughing stock, a pathetic sink. Don, just the thought of what will happen to this wonderful state if Shy

McCloskey loses the primary in September almost makes me want to open this window — notwithstanding the fact that these fucking things are unopenable even on a day as lovely as this one — and jump out. It's a hell almost beyond imagining."

"And you're going to depend on me to change all that? I'm humbled."

"You can help. You can make a difference."

I knew enough about Tom Dunphy — Timothy Callahan's boss, state Assemblyman Myron Lipschutz, had filled me in — to understand that even if the Democrats lost the governorship in November, Dunphy would not be jumping out of any windows. He'd go back to his Manhattan consulting firm and hire himself out to the highest center-left bidder running for office and would pop up periodically as an election-strategy nattering head on CNN and *Morning Joe* and even — Dunphy could both dish it out and take it — Fox News. Armageddon only lasted as long as an election cycle, and The Liberal Rapture was always just around the corner.

I said, "I've never done opposition research before, and generally I disapprove of it."

"Uh-huh."

"From what I understand of the practice, it rarely produces information voters need to know about a candidate. Any news that somebody smoked pot in college or had a love child at seventeen who's now the Norwegian minister of fisheries is basically just a meaningless distraction. Unless, of course, the candidate has made a secret pact with Norway to have all the school children in his jurisdiction eating herring noodle surprise for breakfast and lunch."

A mild shrug. "The stuff you get from oppo's a meaningless distraction, yes, but it's a meaningless distraction that often matters. Elections, as I'm sure you know, are generally won or lost by a few percentage points. And if you can manipulate even a small fraction of voters into being turned off by your opponent's one-time or even current dropping-his-drawers problem, say, or by his having neglected to file his state tax return in a timely manner when he was nine years old, chances are you win. To the sensible folks you and I dine with at La Serre, these rude matters are an irritating distraction, of course. But to that always unhappy segment of the electorate that's eager to focus its inchoate resentments on a public figure who wants something from them — such as a vote — these irrelevancies can reign supreme. Especially if the irrelevancies have to do with things these unhappy voters aren't getting enough of, such as sex or money."

I said, "I've never heard anybody use *inchoate* in conversation before. What were you, an English major?"

Dunphy laughed. "Why else would I end up in a job like this?"

"I know."

"Anyway," he went on, "opposition research can turn up information that's not merely ugly but does in fact bear on character, which is not irrelevant at all for public officials. Example A is one of our own. It was almost certainly a hired investigator such as yourself who tracked down Eliot Spitzer's wayward peregrinations. I know, I know — a man hiring prostitutes. Ideally that ought to be between a man and his wife and his conscience, not for the readership of the *New York Post* to drool over. But our formerly revered crusading Democratic briefly-governor had cracked down on call-girl operations when he was AG, and it was the monumental hypocrisy that was so universally galling. It pains me to say it, but this was a legitimate call by the other side. And think of the closeted gay pols who scorn gay marriage and sexual-orientation job-protection laws, and so on, and then it comes out they've got wide-stance tendencies in airport restrooms. No, matters of character do count — openness, honesty, actually being the person voters are led to think a candidate is. Which brings us, Don, to why I've asked you to come over here today."

"Good."

Dunphy's cell phone warbled, and he picked it up, checked the number and shut the phone off. "That'll wait."

"Thank you."

"Before we proceed, I can assure you that this office has been swept recently for listening and recording devices. Somebody comes in every morning at six. It's Clean-Tech. We use them, and the Republicans use Hunsinger, and Louderbush uses Price. You should know that about Louderbush."

"All right."

"Since what we're about to discuss is extremely 'sensitive'" — Dunphy waggled a set of quotation marks — "and by that I mean very dicey falling-into-the-hands-of-the-media-wise. I would normally ask that you sign a confidentiality agreement. But I'm told that you can be trusted, so a handshake is going to have to do."

"Fine."

"It's your reputation for borderline-difficult, independent-minded integrity, in fact, that got you recommended for this job. That plus, of course, the fact that you are said to be gay as a Greek sailor. That's true, am I right?"

"I've taken it up the butt more than once."

Dunphy grew even pinker. "So you're going to have an entrée into gay circles, and you'll be able to gain the trust of gay people involved in this thing far more reliably than any heterosexual investigator we might have taken on."

I said, "I never heard that about Greek sailors."

"Really?" He looked as if somebody had given him bad information, and what was this going to mean?

"So, what you seem to be getting at, Tom, is that Assemblyman Louderbush is secretly gay? If that's what this is — me outing another closeted pol — I'd have to give that some thought. Louderbush is anti–gay marriage, but otherwise he's not as rabid as a lot of his supporters. He did vote against the hate crimes bill, as I recall. But he's for civil unions, and otherwise he seems to prefer to avoid gay issues altogether. I can think of elected officials far more dangerous to the cause of gay rights than Louderbush.

And there are some of those virulently antigay fellows who — if it was established that they'd had a few call boys up to their hotel rooms for back rubs or for luggage-toting duties on junkets to Ibiza — then I'd be prepared to go to town on the situation. But I don't know about Louderbush. In the hypocrisy department, he wouldn't rank high on most lists."

Dunphy looked somber. "If it was just his being gay, I might agree."

"So he is gay? What else?"

"Here's the deal. If it's true, it's really bad. There's no two ways about it. It is shameful and ugly. Two sources have led us to believe that Louderbush was once in a physically abusive relationship with a young gay man. Louderbush was the abuser. The young man committed suicide — driven to suicide by Louderbush, two of the young man's friends insist. I'm not sure exactly how that would work; it sounds exaggerated. But whatever the truth of the situation, it does seem as if Louderbush was involved in a gay relationship that was messy and ugly and reflects poorly on his character. It was certainly a violation of his marriage vows, not that that alone disqualifies anybody from public office in this easygoing day and age, or should. But it's the physical and emotional cruelty to his boyfriend that — if true — is something I believe voters need to know about before deciding whether or not to cast a ballot for or against Shy McCloskey's primary election opponent."

I thought about what I'd seen and read of Louderbush. "He doesn't come across as mean."

"I agree."

"He's aggressive and noisy on behalf of what he sees as his libertarian principles. But the only people he seems nasty to are elderly people with medical problems. He wants to abolish Medicare, which at this late date has to be considered a sick joke. But that's all ideological and theoretical, and it's hard to imagine Louderbush actually beating up on any individual he's face-to-face with."

"It could be a Jekyll and Hyde type situation with him. This happens."

"I guess."

"If it's not true, of course, we'd pay you for your time and effort, and that would be that. Truth, justice, and the American way would prevail whatever you came up with. But if it is true, well, you'd be doing your bit to help elect a good man governor of our state, and Louderbush could slink away and enter rehab and refind Jesus and live to drive us all nuts another day."

I said, "Okay."

"Okay, what?"

"Okay, I'll do it."

"Excellent."

"I hate this stuff."

"So do I."

"Gay people should be held to the same moral standards for their behavior as other people. But anybody Louderbush's age — what is he, in his fifties? — grew up with so much homophobic crap getting heaped on them, it's a miracle most American homosexuals aren't seething and twisted deep inside. Seething or ashamed."

"Really? Are you?"

"No. I got bored with all that long ago. There's just a bit of residual melancholy."

"Before you start looking into what we've got on Louderbush," Dunphy said, "I should tell you one other thing."

"What?"

"We know that the Republicans have gotten wind of this and they don't want it to come out. They want Louderbush on the Democratic primary ballot. The Ostwind campaign will be working overtime to discredit anything bad you come up with on Louderbush."

"Oh, great."

"They'll say it's all a smear. So you'll need to have all your ducks in a row before we leak this stuff to selected media outlets. Have I whetted your appetite, Don, for your work in the days and weeks ahead?"

I told him no, he hadn't.

CHAPTER TWO

"What do you know about Kenyon Louderbush?" I asked Timmy. I was hiking up State Street hill, and I was one of those people who walk around on sidewalks looking as if they're trying to keep their left ears from falling off. "I mean, besides the obvious."

"You met with Dunphy?"

"Just now."

"So it's Louderbush he wants you to dig up dirt on? Or was that not it?"

"That was it. Opposition research, so-called."

"That's the euphemism."

"Did you ever hear that Louderbush is gay?"

"No, never. And if he is, what else is new? We're almost at that point."

"Not quite. But it's more than gay."

"Oh?"

"It's physical abuse. Supposedly he repeatedly beat up a young gay man he was involved with about five years ago. Don't repeat any of this. It's a horrible thing to say about anybody."

"Of course."

"The young guy, a SUNY student, committed suicide. Supposedly because Louderbush drove him to it. Dunphy wants me to check this out and find out if it's true. And if it is, get the goods and drive Louderbush out of the race."

"How awful."

"They're terrified that all these right-wingers are registering Democratic, and Louderbush will win the primary, and then Ostwind'll bring the Republicans back in. So Louderbush has to go."

"If it's true," Timmy said, "he should go."

"I know. You've never picked up anything in the assembly about Louderbush? You know the scuttlebutt up there."

I was passing the Bank of America now, and the sidewalk was filling up with people heading out for an early lunch. Several other pedestrians were also holding their ears in place and talking, and a few were jabbering away, hands-free, at what looked like no one at all.

Timmy said, "Louderbush is thought of as a conservative Democratic straight arrow. His mostly rural district, out beyond Rochester, is heavily Republican. He's a First Gulf War vet who, I think, unseated a GOP old-timer with senility problems who didn't know when to quit. This was fifteen or so years ago. He rose through the assembly ranks as an antitax zealot — the guy seems to be a genuine libertarian — and then when the Tea Partiers came along, Louderbush was all of a sudden more than just another antigovernment kvetch. He's a good speaker, and he has the right personal résumé: nurse-wife, three personable teenaged kiddos with Silly Bands on their wrists but probably not on their genitalia, and he teaches Sunday school. When the Republicans looked like they were going with the centrist Ostwind, Kenyon suddenly became the answer to the right wing's prayers."

"Teaches Sunday school. Ah, now we're onto something. He's a fanatic."

"No, he's Presbyterian, like you were."

"That's what I mean. They play Guy Lombardo arrangements of Beethoven. On second thought, that's about as violent as Presbyterians generally get."

"Bad enough."

"When I was thirteen, the teen boys' Sunday school teacher, Lawrence McCool, read us sports stories. Heroes, exciting games, sportsmanlike behavior. Mr. McCool was partial to the Yankees, even though central New Jersey had its share of Phillies fans such as myself. There was a prayer before we left the church each week — that's when Jesus elbowed his way in — but the class was mostly sports. Also the odd off-color joke. It was in Sunday school where I first heard the joke whose punch line is, 'Little man of Spic 'n' Span, where were you when the shit hit the fan?'"

"Donald, now I finally grasp what the Reformation was all about."

I passed the Crowne Plaza Hotel. It was in the bar here where some years earlier, when the place was still a Hilton, I interviewed a man in a case that led to my having one of my ears bitten off. The ear was soon re-attached, and now it was practically everybody else out in public who went around apparently in fear of an ear coming loose.

I said, "This afternoon I'm talking to these two people making the accusation against Louderbush. Meanwhile, I'll be in the office googling up what I can on the suicide. Dunphy says what's there is sketchy."

"If it was a SUNY student, you might get something from the school. Although I suppose their records are confidential."

"Yes, I suppose they are."

He heard this the way he often hears things I say, and he briefly moved on to another topic before ringing off.

∫ ∫ ∫ ∫

Gregory Stiver's obit appeared in both the Albany *Times Union* and the Schenectady *Daily Gazette*. Schenectady was where his family lived. The TU also had a brief news story about the suicide.

Stiver, 24, was actually a graduate student in economics — I had imagined someone a bit younger — who had jumped to his death from the roof of the Livingston Quad 4 classroom tower at the State University of New York's Western Avenue campus in Albany. Police had found no evidence of foul play in the late April incident five years earlier. The TU story said friends had described Stiver as despondent in recent weeks. The unnamed friends attributed Stiver's despondency to his inability to line up a job that would follow the awarding of his master's degree in less than a month's time. Two possible teaching jobs had recently fallen through. There was no mention of a troubled romantic relationship nor of any physical abuse.

The Schenectady obituary described a life that offered no hint that it might come to a sad and early end. Stiver had been an excellent student in Schenectady public schools. He'd been a member of the debating club in high school and had been on the swim team. He had earned a bachelor's degree in economics at SUNY Albany two years before his death. At SUNY, Stiver had been active in the Federalist Society, the conservative constitutional "originalists" — and also in the Log Cabin Club, the gay Republicans. So he was conservative, he was gay, and he was out.

The photo accompanying the Schenectady obit was a head shot, perhaps a student ID picture, of a pleasant-faced young man with a crew cut and a wide smile. He seemed to be wearing a jacket and tie, an unusual getup for a college student in our casual era.

Stiver was survived, both obits said, by his parents, Anson and Margery Stiver of Schenectady, and by a brother, Hugh, and a sister, Jennifer, also of Schenectady.

A funeral was scheduled to take place at the Fairlawn Presbyterian Church in Schenectady. In lieu of flowers, donations could be made to something called The Eddie Fund, in care of the funeral home.

That's all the Internet had to offer on Gregory Stiver. I googled the Eddie Fund, but nothing came up. Either it was so obscure or so old-fashioned that it had no Internet presence, or sometime during the previous five years the Eddie Fund had ceased to exist. It wasn't in the phone book, either.

§ § § §

Virgil Jackman and Janie Insinger had had some sort of falling out, Dunphy had told me. The former friends were no longer speaking to each other, so I was going to have to interview them separately. In fact, I preferred this. I could listen to their own versions of events, cross-check them, and do re-interviews if needed.

Already the two accusers had credibility because both had contacted the McCloskey campaign independently with the same story about a physically abusive Kenyon Louderbush having driven Greg Stiver to suicide. Insinger had also called the Merle Ostwind campaign, she told Dunphy, because she was so angry with Louderbush that she was determined that all of his political opponents should gang up on him and keep him from gaining higher office. Insinger told Dunphy that she had not gone to the press with her charges because she wanted her name kept out of the controversy for family and professional reasons. Exposing Louderbush would have to be left up to individuals of a certain ilk such as myself.

I wasn't sure how it would be possible to confirm and expose Louderbush's reprehensible behavior if one of the two witnesses to it refused to be named. I would have to figure that out; maybe other witnesses could be found and they would be willing to speak out. Dunphy said that if I were to become convinced of Louderbush's guilt, he was ready to approach Louderbush privately — no press leakage at this point — and urge him to save himself from public embarrassment over what we had dug up and drop out of the race. Dunphy told me he would consider this an act of patriotism, not extortion. The US Attorney's interpretation of any such conversation might be harsher, however, and I told Dunphy we needed to find a less indictable way to shove Louderbush off the Democratic ticket. He asked me if I had a law degree, and I admitted that, no, I was just another English major. This gave him pause. He said he knew a lawyer he could ask, and he would do that.

∫ ∫ ∫ ∫

Virgil Jackman was taking a late lunch break at two o'clock from his job as an assistant manager at a chain sporting goods store in the Colonie Mall, and I met him at the Denny's on Wolf Road. He was easy to spot from Dunphy's description: a good six-five with a bodybuilder's physique under his retailer's dress shirt and name tag, wide gray eyes, and an interestingly meaty face with a small shrub of dark blond goatee at the bottom of it, the only thing delicate about him.

The place had thinned out after the noon-to-two rush, and we asked for and were led to a corner booth in the nearly deserted far end of the restaurant.

"I'm glad you're here. I didn't think anybody was gonna call me back," Jackman said, "and that was starting to piss me off. I thought about calling the Republicans, but my dad was IUE, a shop steward, and he'd ream my ass if I helped out those management types."

"That's a union?"

"International Union of Electrical Workers. Dad had thirty-five years in at Schenectady GE when they shut down his division five years before he was set to retire. Now he works security at Sears during the week and Home Depot on weekends. Those aren't union shops, for sure, but Dad is still party all the way — campaigned for Obama, African-American no problem. So I can hear him screaming his head off if I even picked up the phone and dialed a Republican."

The waitress came over, and Jackman ordered a taco salad and an iced tea, and I said those also sounded good to me.

"I know Shy McCloskey has a lot of union endorsements," I said.

"Yeah, that's good. Glad to help out this guy."

"But I'm curious. What if the union endorsee had been the bad guy here? Would you still have exposed his bad behavior?"

"Sure, I would. What was done to Greg was pathetic. It was a sin, and it was a crime. The idea that a guy who would do a thing like that could be the governor makes me sick. So, I'd be pissed even if he was one of our guys."

"How was what Louderbush did a crime? You mean assault?"

"Sure. If I smacked you around even if it's just some roughhousing, if you said stop and I keep it up, that's assault.

Even just touching a person if it's unwanted is assault."

"You know the law on this stuff."

"Yeah. I do. My sister's ex-husband. He used to hit her, and I tried to deal with him on my own. Big mistake. Just call the cops is what I should have done."

"So you have a record?"

"Expunged after one year. I learned my lesson."

The iced tea arrived. An elderly couple hobbled our way and planted themselves in the adjoining booth. "This catsup needs wiped off," the old lady told our waitress, who removed the offending Heinz container.

"So, tell me, Virgil. How did you know Greg Stiver? He was no union man from what I've read about him."

"I lived in the next-door apartment on Allen Street. I mean, Janie Insinger and I did. We broke up after she decided she was a lesbian, although now she's with a guy again. Some ex-marine. I thought about telling the guy Janie is gonna be nothing but trouble, but I'm dating now myself, and Kimberly says leave it alone, just stay out of it, and I'm sure she's correct. We ran into them one time at a club and everybody ignored each other."

"Janie also contacted the McCloskey campaign, as I guess you know."

"We aren't on speaking terms, but she left a message saying she was gonna call you guys, and I should, too. I was gonna anyways. Kenyon Louderbush has no business going around running for governor and acting like he's some nice guy with a wife and kids. Not after what he did to Greg Stiver."

"What did he do? Tell me what you saw and heard."

The old couple in the next booth were sitting silently and could have been listening to our every word, and Jackman leaned forward and said quietly but distinctly, "Louderbush would beat the shit out of Greg at least once a week. We didn't know Greg real well, but he gave Janie and I a ride to school on Mondays and Wednesdays, and if Louderbush was there the night before

— and we could always hear the crashing around and the yelling — Greg would be all beat up the next day. He had a big bruise one time, and his lip was bleeding on another occasion that I remember. One time he asked me to drive his car because he said his head hurt so much he thought he might have a concussion. Janie and I both said, hey, you shouldn't let this guy get away with this; you don't deserve to be treated this way. And Greg would always say he didn't want to get the guy in trouble, and sometimes he'd laugh and say this is what he deserves for getting involved with a married man."

The old folks seated next to us seemed frozen in place, and were either studying the menu with fierce concentration or they were taking in everything Jackman said and would have an exciting time hashing it over later in the car.

"How did you know the identity of the man who visited Stiver and beat him?"

"We saw him in the hall lots of times, and I recognized him from the news. One time I even said to him, 'Hi Senator.' I wanted him to know I knew who he was, and I thought that might make him think twice before he beat up on Greg again. But these guys think they own the world, and they can get away with anything they want."

"Louderbush is an assemblyman, not senator. Could you be confusing him with someone else?"

"No, we used to see him all the time on the eleven o'clock news. He was the guy who was always blah-blah-ing about taxes. Hey, I'm against taxes like anybody else. But how else are you going to pay for the fire department and so forth? Are we all supposed to put our own fire out?"

"And Greg acknowledged to you that he was in fact having an affair with Assemblyman Louderbush?"

"Yeah, when I said Janie and I recognized him, Greg was cool with that. He said don't tell anybody, that Louderbush would just deny it, but that Louderbush was his boyfriend. Louderbush came to one of Greg's econ classes one time, and then he came onto him afterward, and they got started. Greg said he really admired the guy, and the fact that he was this big Republican was a real turn-on. I guess he thought Louderbush was attractive, too. I know if I was into guys, I wouldn't want some fifty-year-old old fart like that getting all over me."

"Sure."

"I'd want a young athlete. One time Janie and I tried a three-way with this college wrestler we met at a club, and that was kind of a turn-on for me. But the woman would've had to be there. Otherwise, what's the point?"

"How long did the relationship last between Louderbush and Stiver?"

"From fall till Greg killed himself in April. Greg was getting more and more upset and worried that he wasn't getting a teaching job or anything else coming down the pike. Then he had this asshole pounding on him every time Louderbush came over and they had a few drinks, and I guess he just cracked. You'd have to be pretty much at the end of your rope to get you to jump off of a building. I don't know how anybody could make themselves do that. It goes against all your instincts."

"So alcohol was an important part of the relationship between Stiver and Louderbush?"

"I think it was more Louderbush. He'd have to have a drink to loosen up, Greg said. Then they'd get it on, and then Louderbush would have another drink or two, and that's when he'd go off and get physical. At first, when we asked him about the crashing noises and the yelling, Greg would just say, no, there was no problem, that they just fell or something. Later on, he admitted what was really going on, and he said he tried to get Louderbush to cut it out. But he also said that deep down he was only getting what he needed. He said his old man beat him when he was a kid, and now apparently there was something in his psychology that made him like getting hurt by some man. He admitted that this was true."

"Was Greg in psychotherapy? It sounds as if he had some

real understanding of why he put up with the way Louderbush treated him."

"Janie actually tried to get him to go, but he never would, I don't think."

The waitress arrived with our taco salads, and the old woman in the next booth said to her, "We would like to order now. We have been waiting for quite some time."

"Sorry. I'll be right with you."

"We got here before those two men did, and they already have their food."

The waitress, a squat, buxom young black woman, carefully ignored this. "I can take your order now. What would you like to order, ma'am?"

The couple proceeded to order eggs Benedict. The waitress explained that Denny's didn't have any of those, so then the couple decided to make do with a single grilled cheese sandwich served on two plates. After that was settled, I asked Jackman more questions.

"Both you and your former girlfriend have told the McCloskey campaign that you believe Kenyon Louderbush drove Greg Stiver to suicide. That's a serious charge to make against anybody. Stiver was a grown-up. He was free to make choices. He could have told Louderbush to take a hike. He could even have called the police and charged Louderbush with assault. He could have done a lot of things to get out of the mess he was in. Louderbush did not in fact shove Stiver off that building. You can attest that this was an abusive relationship, but that's a far as you can go, I think, when it comes to pinning anything on Kenyon Louderbush.

"If you are going to go public with this — as Tom Dunphy says you're willing to do — you might want to describe what you saw and heard, and you can of course relay what Greg told you about the relationship. But you can expect people to challenge your contention that Louderbush drove Greg Stiver to take his own life — *drove* is the word you seem determined to use — and you'll have to be ready for disagreements and other interpretations coming at you from many directions. And a lot of people who disagree with you are going to act very hostile."

Jackman was cracking off portions of taco shell and gathering up little heaps of meat, lettuce, sauce, and sour cream, and shoveling it all into his large face. Through a mouthful of this stuff, he said, "I saw the suicide note."

"You did? How?"

"It was on the kitchen table. Mrs. Pensivy, the landlady, let us into Greg's apartment before the police came over. Somebody at SUNY called her. There was a note in Greg's handwriting on the table, and it said, 'I hurt too much.'"

"That's all it said?"

"Janie started to cry. Mrs. Pensivy, too."

"It didn't mention Kenyon Louderbush?"

"It didn't have to."

"What happened to the note?"

"The cops must have taken it."

"Did anyone else see it?"

"I wouldn't think so."

"Did Mrs. Pensivy know about the abuse?"

"Not as far as I know. She lived next door with her sister."

"Who else knew about the beatings?"

Jackman mulled this over. "Greg never said. But other people must have figured it out. At school, or his family. You could see the marks and what have you. He had a big shiner one time. Janie gave him a cube steak to press against it."

"Did Greg ever seek medical treatment that you know of?"

"Just from Janie and I. The cube steak."

"I thought people only treated black eyes with steak in the comics. Dagwood, or Nancy and Sluggo."

A puzzled look. "What are those? You mean like in newspapers?"

"Yes."

"My granddad still reads the *Times Union* most of the time. Sports and what have you."

I supposed the couple in the next booth could have explained what the funny papers used to mean in American life, but the old man and the old woman were busy staring intently at each other's sagging midsections, and I didn't break their reverie and bring them into our discussion.

CHAPTER THREE

"And I was like, I *have* to say something, and Kev was like, no you *don't* have to say anything, just let Virgil do it, cuz nobody's going to give him any shit, cuz he's a guy. But it just didn't seem right that if I know about this guy, I should just let him get elected governor of New York, and anyway maybe he still beats up on people. He could, you know, go after some young guy who works in his office — put the moves on him and then beat on him the way he did with Greg. My conscience would bother me if I didn't speak out, although I don't want my name mentioned, and I think you can understand the reason why."

"Tom Dunphy said it was for family and professional reasons."

"That's right. My parents would shit burritos if I did anything to mess up Kenyon Louderbush's chance to win the election. They think he's Jesus Walks on Water, and they don't know about the gay stuff or any of that. Also, at work it would not be appreciated if I got into some political thing. That is strictly, like, no way."

"Where do you work, Janie?"

"Walmart. I'm an assistant shift supervisor. I keep the associates happy and productive."

"I see."

We were seated in a booth at the bar at the Outback Steakhouse not far from the Wolf Road Denny's where I had my late lunch with Virgil Jackman. Insinger had gotten off work at four, and she was sipping some wacky concoction: half a tumbler of Red Bull, a shot of rum, and a cocktail onion bobbing in it. I was nursing a Sam Adams and eating too many peanuts coated with corn syrup shellac.

It was hard to imagine Insinger supervising the impoverished geezers and laid-off math teachers at Walmart who wandered the aisles hanging red sale tags of $7.99 on garments sewn on the outskirts of Kunming for twenty-five cents each. With her croaky voice and *cuzes* and *was likes*, Insinger seemed like an implausible boss lady at a company famed for both cracking the whip and inspiring near-religious awe in its employees. Her deficiencies may have been compensated for to some extent by her appearance. Insinger was a knockout, both svelte and sweetly busty, with a pert nose, large hazel eyes and a lower lip the size of a kielbasa. She was done up in the tart-wear that the young routinely leave home in now, making little distinction between going to work and attending a backroom sex club. It had been a while since I had generated a physical response to a body of the opposite sex, but there was something about Insinger's appearance and her perfume — peony bloom? — that combined to have me shifting in my seat. Until, that is, she opened her mouth again.

"So I was like, hey, if I can't personally screw over this dickhead senator and keep my job, I can at least make sure somebody else does it. After all, the guy's practically a murderer. Don't you agree?"

"In a sense, yes, if what you say is true. What is it exactly that you are saying? What did you see and hear that led you to make this accusation?"

She hesitated. "First, I have to ask you something."

"Okay."

"Are you, like, recording this conversation?"

"No, I'm not."

"I'm only asking because my boss says to be careful about that type of situation. You can never be sure, she says. You should always just figure that somebody might be wearing a wire."

"Your boss at Walmart told you this? Or do you also work for the Central Intelligence Agency?"

"No, of course not. But it could be the government or some lawyer who's gonna sue the company."

I said, "Even if I was recording our conversation, might that not actually be helpful to you? In case there's any confusion later on about what you said to me."

Insinger slurped up some of her scarlet refreshment and glanced around the room. No one was seated nearby, and the few people in other booths and at the bar seemed to be taking no notice of us.

"It's just that…this whole thing is making me kind of nervous. Oh, I know, I know. This was my idea. I was the one who called up. But, like, this guy is a senator. Those people do not appreciate getting screwed over."

"Assemblymen don't have their own militias or goon squads. I wouldn't worry about that."

"No, I mean they can just pick up the phone. And then all of a sudden your income tax is overdue or your car insurance is no good. I know a girl who crossed this dude who works for the Albany water department, and now she gets speeding tickets all the time."

"It's up to you whether or not you want to go ahead with this, Janie. I've already got Virgil's version of events. It would be helpful, though, if you would just confirm or maybe add something to what I've already been told. I understand that you and Virgil were Greg Stiver's neighbors on Allen Street."

She nodded.

"And you knew Greg casually?"

"Yeah."

"You rode out to SUNY with him twice a week?"

"Yeah. But wait a minute. I have to ask you something."

"Go ahead."

"Did Virgil badmouth me?"

"No, he spoke of you with tender affection."

She laughed. "You're a freakin' liar."

"Okay. He said you left him for a woman, and that you were a lot of trouble."

"I did *not* leave him for a woman. I left him because he was always trying to get another guy into bed with us. I did it one time, and then I got creeped out. I think Virgil has some issues he hasn't worked out. Anyway, Lori Wroble is my friend, not my girlfriend."

"Either would be okay in my book."

"I've tried gay sex, sure, but something was definitely missing. Not with Lori, I don't mean. I prefer guys, and I started to wonder if maybe Virgil does too. God, should I be mentioning this?"

"Up to you. But I'm mainly interested in Greg Stiver and his relationship with Kenyon Louderbush."

She rolled her eyes. "Now Greg, that poor guy was *totally* gay. What I didn't get was, a guy that attractive, why didn't he have a nice boyfriend his own age, somebody who treated him with respect? Greg was kind of straight — I don't mean sexually — but very sort of... serious. He was very political. Very conservative. He had a lot to say about that stuff if you gave him half a chance. Sometimes in the car I would just, like, tune out. It was *blabbedy-blah*, *blabbedy-blah*. Bush was driving the country into an economic ditch. *Bush* was! And Bush was a Republican! I hate to think what Greg would say about Obama. Oh my God."

"Apparently it was Louderbush's and Greg's politics that were part of the attraction the two had for each other. Was that your impression?"

"I guess so. Why else would Greg get involved with an older man? Especially a guy who was married with kids? But it was also, like, low self-esteem. Greg told us about how his dad used to beat on him when he was a kid. And when Mr. Louderbush pounded him around, this was just what he was used to and even had it coming. It was really sad. Greg was one mixed-up puppy."

I asked Insinger about the pattern of abuse as she had heard it through the walls of her adjoining apartment and as Greg had described it to her and Jackman.

"It was always kind of late," she said. "Virgil and I would be studying or chilling out or whatever, and we'd hear them going at it. Yelling and banging around and breaking stuff. Sometimes we talked about going over or even calling the cops. We waited, though — we decided to mind our own business — and then we asked Greg about it one day, and at first he said oh no, nothing was going on, don't get your thong in an uproar. Then later he finally did admit they were fighting, but he told us to never mind, he would be okay. He was afraid of getting Louderbush in trouble, I could tell."

"Afraid?"

"Well, yeah. I mean, Louderbush was this extremely successful big hotshot. If Greg ruined his life or told his wife or put it on Facebook or something, who knows what might happen?"

"Did he say Louderbush threatened him?"

Insinger picked up a shiny peanut and popped it into her mouth. "No. He never said that straight out." She glanced around the bar, and so did I. Nobody was within earshot of us, and nobody seemed to be paying us any attention.

"When the two men were yelling at each other, were you ever able to make out anything anyone said?"

"Hmm. One time somebody screamed, 'You can eat shit!' I think it was Louderbush. It was a lot of that kind of drunk yelling. They'd get liquored up and start in. I have to say, I'm a little surprised Greg didn't defend himself more. Senator Louderbush was big and strong, Greg said, but he was older, too. Virgil asked Greg one time if he ever hit Louderbush back, and Greg just said no, it was a sin to hit a Republican. He was being funny, but I think he really was, like, kind of scared to get in this guy's face. Maybe he'd get Greg kicked out of SUNY or his degree would be a blank sheet of paper or something."

"Did Greg ever talk about taking his own life?"

Insinger grew thoughtful. "I don't know."

"I mean to you or Virgil."

"Sometimes he said he was worn out."

"Uh-huh."

"He'd be really, really tired, and he'd have this kind of what's-the-use? attitude. But then a couple of days later he'd be, like, oh-fine. Right before he died, Greg was really down in one of his moods. A total mope-head. But that was mainly because he got turned down by two colleges for teaching jobs. One in Connecticut, one out near Rochester, which was his first choice. He didn't know what he was going to do after he got his master's, and he had these huge student loans. I was a senior then, and I knew how he felt, though this was before Obama fucked up the economy, and five years ago there were still jobs in retailing, thank God. Virgil and I both got jobs right after we graduated and got into management career tracks. Today we'd both be, like, out selling our butts on a street corner in Arbor Hill."

"Assemblyman Louderbush represents a district near Rochester. Was Greg hoping to live near him?"

"Oh. He didn't say. But he wouldn't have said anything. Not to Virgil and me. He knew we disapproved and that we thought the relationship was self-destructive for Greg."

I said, "I understand you saw the suicide note."

"Yeah. It was so sad. I cried. Even Virgil teared up. Mrs. Pensivy cried her heart out."

"The landlady."

"She lived next door, but she let us in before the cops came. Somebody called her who she knew at SUNY."

"And the note said — what was it?"

"'I hurt too much.' So sad, so sad."

"And you recognized Greg's handwriting?"

"Yeah."

"Where had you seen his handwriting before?"

"Oh, hmm. I guess when he taped a note to our door about rides or whatever."

"What became of the suicide note?"

"The cops took it, I guess."

"How can you be sure that Greg's suicide was directly related to Kenyon Louderbush? It's plain that he was a source of stress and confusion and pain in Greg's life. But it also sounds as if Greg thought that the relationship had some kind of future. Greg's attempt to move to Louderbush's assembly district is an indication of that. You and Virgil told the McCloskey campaign that you thought Louderbush drove Greg to suicide. Wasn't that the term you both used?"

"Yeah."

"How could you be so certain?"

"Well, jeez. I mean, like, if you were involved with a person who was giving you a black eye once or twice a week and making your lip hang off and bleed all over, and you just couldn't help yourself and get away, and you didn't know any other way out, wouldn't you think about just ending it all? When life is a living hell, and the person who is making it that way won't back off, it's just what people do sometimes."

"But is that 'driving' someone to suicide? It's not clear-cut. There are alternatives."

"Well, it's clear enough cut to me. What do you want, for me to draw you a freakin' diagram?"

CHAPTER FOUR

I thought Jackman and Insinger both might have been right that in a real enough sense Assemblyman Louderbush "drove" Greg Stiver to suicide. At a minimum, Louderbush preyed on Stiver's vulnerabilities, cruelly manipulated him psychologically, and treated him sadistically — and illegally. If Jackman's and Insinger's description of events was accurate, Louderbush was a man of despicable character who was unfit for public office, even in a country with traditionally low standards of electability. While the American electorate was often at home with officials who had some outsider-y rough edges — rampant infidelity, expense-account ambiguity, a DUI or two — violently unstable men ordinarily did not receive a pass from voters.

And yet the situation remained murky. While Virgil Jackman was willing to sign an affidavit attesting to Louderbush's physical abuse and said he would "go on Liz Bishop" — a Schenectady TV news anchor — if asked to do so, Insinger said she wanted her name kept out of it. Her parents would not want her in the public eye in a matter of such heated controversy, and neither would Walmart.

From the Outback parking lot, I phoned Dunphy.

"Tom, this may take some time. I'm going to need more to go on than what Jackman and Insinger are offering. They're both credible enough for our purposes, but Insinger doesn't want her name used, and Jackman's family has union ties — his dad was an IUE shop steward — and that'll have the Louderbush people yelling foul. I'd like to keep digging and see if I can come up with some other people who will corroborate Insinger's and Jackman's allegations and are willing to do it publicly."

"Go for it. I told Shy that you were on Louderbush's case, and he is positively thrilled that you're taking this on."

"Good."

"He is so disgusted by the abuse story and the suicide of

a gay young man that he asked if it might be possible to have Louderbush prosecuted. I'm not sure what the statute of limitations would be on that, but I'm going to have our legal guys and gals look into it."

"If it's all true, sure."

"Just work fast. It's three months till the primary, and we're all strapped to the ass of a charging rhinoceros. Our TV ad campaign for the primary launches just after the Fourth of July, and it would be just loverly if we could scrap all that and husband our ever-too-meager resources for the general. Get Louderbush the fuck out of the way, and we can save a pile of dough *and* sail past Merle into the governor's mansion. Think you can do it, Don? From what I've heard about you, I'm betting you can."

Dunphy liked to lay it on. "If I can save you hundreds of thousands of dollars in television ad buys," I said, "maybe I should be working on a percentage basis. Twenty-five percent of whatever you would have spent."

His breathy pause suggested he thought I was serious. "That would possibly be against the law, but I'm sure a bonus above and beyond your reasonable fee might be doable. Maybe five K. Or something in that neighborhood."

"Thanks, but let's see what I come up with."

"Of course."

It occurred to me that Dunphy might be recording our conversation. This would have been illegal in itself since Dunphy had not informed me he was doing so. But he had never met me before that day, and he probably didn't fully trust Myron Lipschutz and whoever else in the party had recommended me.

I said, "Assuming I get the goods on Louderbush's rotten behavior and then you go the media-leak route as opposed to the privately-confront-Louderbush route, I want this to be air-tight. Even cable news will be wary of a story as incendiary as this, so it's essential, I think, that I find more witnesses willing to go public with what they know. In the Spitzer case, how was the initial leak handled?"

Dunphy hesitated and seemed to be choosing his words carefully, and now I was convinced that our conversation was going straight into a recorder. "Nobody knows for sure exactly how it was done. The guys at the *Times* and the *Post* who broke the story aren't talking as to who their sources were. But the assumption is that private investigators hired by Sam Krupa, the old GOP dirty tricks guy, followed the gov when he walked into post offices to buy untraceable money orders to pay off his K-an-hour gal-pals. Other operatives bribed hotel workers. They had names and places and dates, and they checked this stuff against the governor's official schedule, and it all jibed. Then they found a prosecutor in Miami who was eager to make history by busting one of the entrepreneurial gals and offering her a deal if she named the governor. Then Krupa leaked word of the official investigation, and the caped crusader's cook was goosed."

"But there's no official investigation of Louderbush underway," I said. "So the witnesses we offer up have to be a hundred percent credible, and the more of them there are, the better."

"I agree."

"So who hired Sam Krupa to bring down Spitzer? The Wall Street guys he'd gone after as AG?"

"That's the common assumption. Nobody is admitting to it. The big bank guys hated him to the depths of their tainted souls. Spitzer inspired such rage in the financial community that any number of those people would have done just about anything to bring about his comeuppance. In the end — an end that gathered itself soon after he took office and then fell upon the governor with the speed of light — in the end, his enemies didn't need hit men or sabotage or the political equivalent of tactical nuclear weapons to finish him off. It was death by floozy, that most commonplace of downfalls. Who would have thought? Who in *hell* would have thought?"

"It's a compelling enough story," I said, "but it has something the Louderbush situation lacks so far, and that is direct participants in the misdeeds of the accused who are willing to offer first-hand testimony. Some of Spitzer's call girls and their employers talked in the end, but Greg Stiver is dead and unable to do that. So you'll need more to go on, and that's my job at this point."

"It is indeed."

"I'm going to work on this because (a) you are paying me, but also because (b) Louderbush's crime is far worse than Eliot Spitzer's. Hubris and a wayward dick are serious misdemeanors in a political context, but assault is just plain rotten and indefensible. Especially when it's an older person beating on a young and vulnerable person over a period of time. If Louderbush did what Jackman and Insinger claim he did, even if it didn't lead directly to Stiver's suicide, he should be run out of office and maybe, if it's not too late, into jail."

Standing next to my Toyota near the sparsely utilized rear of the Outback parking lot, I was aware that a dark-colored SUV with tinted windows had pulled in next to me and three men had quickly gotten out of it. One immediately ripped the phone out of my hand as another whacked me in the back of both knees with something metallic.

As I was going down, a third man pounded my face with a leather-gloved fist. The pain that roared through me was so overwhelming that I was surprised there was still room for the intensity of the nausea that hit a millisecond later. The three were kicking me now on the back and shoulders, and at my midsection whenever it was exposed. I fought back through a fog of blood, but these three were as coordinated in their joint efforts as the New York Giants, except they seemed larger and meaner.

I rolled and tried to protect my head as more blows were struck, and I managed to get part of my lower body under a vehicle before I realized it was theirs and they might climb back into the thing and drive over me. I tried to wriggle free again and was aided in this effort by grabbing an ankle and hanging onto it while its owner attempted to wrench himself free. The man was wearing finely made summer-weight dark wool slacks and his excellently crafted shoes had been nicely shined, if now scuffed.

Somebody else kicked me hard on the side of my head, and then I saw red and left all my cares behind.

CHAPTER FIVE

I said, "What happened to my Blackberry?"

"Somebody picked it up. I have it."

Timmy was in the chair next to my bed, and at the foot of the bed Dunphy had planted himself in a wheelchair he had dragged in from the corridor on the sixth floor D-wing at Albany Med.

Dunphy said, "Don't worry about using your phone anytime soon. Just concentrate on healing. Even if you're out of here later today, take a day or three to regroup. Obviously the situation is urgent, but the most important thing you can do for all of us at this point is for you to be able to function at one hundred percent."

"Nothing's broken," I said. "No concussion either, apparently. I'm just scraped up and bruised all over and sore as shit, and my head hurts where they mangled my bad ear. That ear has been through it: D-Day, the siege of Hue, Albany politics."

"You can't hear very well through that bandage," Timmy said. "Shouldn't you wait until the bandage comes off before you try to work again?"

"What?"

"You heard me."

"Exactly."

I said to Dunphy, "Timmy tells me that Jackman and Insinger are both okay. Nobody went after them. And they have protection now?"

"Some discreet security guys for when they leave work. Jackman we had to talk into it, but Insinger was grateful. Budgetwise the campaign can't legitimately pick this up at this point, but some friends of Shy have stepped up to the plate, no problem."

I pointed at the curtain behind Timmy. "Anybody in that

other bed?"

"He died overnight," Timmy said. "And elderly man from Scotia."

"Oh."

"What did you tell the cops?" Dunphy asked. "They haven't been in touch with us, so I assume we're keeping them out of it at this point? And I do think it's preferable that they remain out of the loop for the time being."

"A police dick I know was in a while ago, Bill Hanratty. I told him I was working on something but preferred not to say what. He knows I consort with dubious types such as yourself, Tom, so he wasn't surprised to see me banged up, and he was okay with letting it ride for now. Anyhow, he's a humble cop who's busy with your garden-variety apolitical criminals, and he feels no deep need to involve himself in the glamorous world of democracy-at-work savagery."

"Hanratty did talk to a couple of witnesses," Timmy said, "who Don plans to interview."

"Witnesses to the attack?"

"The tail end of it apparently. Three guys who work for an insurance office up Wolf Road. If they hadn't come out of the restaurant just then, the beaters might have gotten some more licks in. I was lucky. The attackers took off when these insurance guys saw what was going on and one of them took out his cell, Hanratty said, and got 911."

"This could have been so much worse," Timmy said, squeezing my arm. "I'm the one who's still shaky when I think about that."

I said, "Ouch."

"Sorry."

"What's interesting was how they seemed to know exactly what they were doing in the sense of inflicting pain but minimal permanent damage. They hit the backs of my legs but not my kneecaps. They smacked me good on the upper back but not lower down where they could have messed up any number of organs. The head stuff was nasty. It knocked me out, and it bloodied my scalp and messed up my ear. But the hits were glancing. These guys were not trying to kill me or even wreck me for life. It was more of a violent warning."

"But they didn't say anything?" Dunphy asked.

"Not a word. It was as if they knew I knew why this was happening."

"Are you working on any other cases this could be related to?"

"No, just routine stuff. Missing ex-husbands and girlfriends, some insurance scams, a township pilfering thing involving probable theft of road department fuel supplies. This thing is related to the Louderbush situation, I'm pretty sure. My question is, though, why did whoever it was go after me and not Jackman and Insinger? Why warn me off and not them? I'm replaceable in this equation. Any number of Manhattan PIs I know of could handle it, but the two witnesses to Louderbush's crimes are central. Yet nobody's laid a finger on them. There has to be a reason for that."

"Both of them were upset when we told them what had happened," Dunphy said. "Especially Insinger. She said Walmart doesn't like violence."

"Did the TU have anything? Or the TV stations?"

Timmy said, "Not so far. If it had been somebody's house pet who got mauled, TV would be all over it."

Dunphy asked me if I had gotten a good look at the attackers, and I said I hadn't. "I doubt if I could pick them out of a lineup. What I can say is, they were tall, beefy guys, thirtyish or thereabouts, and two looked kind of Slavic maybe. Serbian? Or am I just reading that into it from news photos of Ratko Mladic? One was a bit darker. Not black. Brownish, though not Hispanic probably. Gypsy possibly."

Timmy said, "Roma."

"Okay."

"It's what they prefer to be called."

"Well, far be it for me. I hope I run into this guy again so I can apologize."

Timmy told Dunphy, "A writer friend once told me that I have the soul of a copy editor. I took it as a compliment."

Uncertain of what to make of this two-acerbic-gay-guys-in-love back-and-forth, Dunphy said, "So the insurance-guy witnesses must have gotten a look at the car the baddies were driving, no?"

"Hanratty says it was a black Lincoln Navigator with Jersey tags. The three witnesses disagreed on what the numbers were. If this was a higher priority case, the cops might fool around with different number combinations and try to match them with New Jersey Navigators. But they don't have a lot of extra time on their hands, and of course the Albany Police Department is unaware that what I am working on is destined to alter the course of Empire State history."

Timmy said, "Lincoln Navigators aren't your usual Jersey goon style of vehicle. Or are they? They're usually the mode of transport of magnates, rock stars, the Secret Service."

"These guys could have been any of the above. Come to think of it, they were all nattily clad — upscale smart casual."

"Those blood stains will be hard to get out," Timmy said. "Their slacks will probably need dry cleaning."

"And there I was writhing on the tarmac outside Outback in my togs from Marshalls. Maybe I was attacked for my questionable taste."

"It wouldn't have been the first time."

Dunphy said, "You guys sure are taking this a lot more lightly than I would have. I'd be shitting my pants and probably going into hiding. Anyway, I'm grateful you're willing to stick this out, Don. It shows you know how important this project is and that you're willing to do what's... I hate to sound sloppy, but the word that comes to mind is *patriotic*."

Timmy and I exchanged glances, and I said to Dunphy, "It's

true this is a job I don't think I need to be embarrassed about. Not so far. But you know, one thing you might be able to help me out with, Tom, is this: Who besides you and Shy McCloskey knew that I agreed just yesterday morning to take this Louderbush thing on? And who besides you knew I was meeting Jackman and Insinger yesterday afternoon? It seems odd that anybody working for Louderbush — if that's who we're looking at here — would have learned so quickly of my plans and of my whereabouts. I keep trying to figure that out. It's puzzling."

Timmy and I both looked at Dunphy. He had been sitting with his elegantly shod feet on the metal footrests of his wheelchair, and now he shifted and placed both feet on the floor. "You're right. How did these guys know?"

"It's disturbing."

"Yeah."

"Either Jackman or Insinger could have let something slip. Although, I set up my appointments with them only a few hours before I met them. There wasn't much time for either of them to mention me to anybody casually and innocently. Either of them, of course, could have done it intentionally — set me up for whatever weird unknown malign reason. But when I met them, both struck me as sincere in their strong disapproval of Kenyon Louderbush and his actions, and highly unlikely to be reporting secretly to him or his staff or his Serbian militia."

"You're right."

"It's baffling."

"All I can say, Don, is that I certainly have not discussed your working for us with anybody except Shy. And he was unaware of the specifics of your meetings yesterday until after they took place and you landed in here."

"What about your staff? Beryl and her crew out there?"

"They don't even know who the fuck you are. You're just some security guy."

"Right."

"What about Myron Lipschutz?" Dunphy asked. "Timothy, your boss."

"He knows Don is working for you, but not that it's about Louderbush. And Myron certainly didn't know Don was meeting yesterday with Jackman and Insinger."

I said, "And you're sure your phone lines are clean? And your office? What about your computers?"

"Absolutely. The computers are checked for hackers, and the rooms and phone lines are swept every morning just before Beryl gets in."

"By Clean-Tech?"

"Yes."

"And they're trustworthy? The company isn't owned by Diebold Incorporated. or Karl Rove's brother-in-law in Florida?"

Dunphy screwed up his pink face. "Jesus, you're making me nervous, Don. If you can't trust the firms you pay the big bucks to secure your information, who can you trust?"

"You don't by chance record telephone conversations yourself, do you, Tom?"

"Me? Why would I?"

CHAPTER SIX

My head hurt. The doctors said I wasn't concussed — no unsteadiness, no disorientation, nothing untoward on the MRI — but every beat of my heart was like a sledgehammer against my cranium.

"Now I know what a circus tent stake feels like when those apelike guys take turns pounding it into the ground," I told Timmy.

"Funny, I think of tent stakes as insensate. But maybe it's because they don't have mouths that we never hear their pitiful cries."

"When was my last Tylenol?"

"Six thirty. You'd better wait another little while. I guess a beer wouldn't help at this point. Or a medicinal bit of weed."

"Nah."

I was in bed at our house on Crow Street. When I'd gotten home just after five, Timmy had warmed up some tam yam gai he'd picked up at the Thai place on Lark Street and I sat at the kitchen table and ate it. Such an improvement over the hospital boiled-chicken-in-mucus. I went up to lie down then and make some calls on my cell, but at first the throbbing was just too disconcerting. Looking at TV was out of the question — MSNBC is not the answer to a headache — so I tried some Art Tatum. That was too busy for the state of my tender brain, and Timmy put on a Bach partita, but that was even busier.

I tried silence for a while, thinking I might drift off to sleep, but then I kept wondering who it was who had set me up, and my mind was so busy chewing over that question that soon I was wide awake.

While Timmy filled in the answers to the *Times* crossword puzzle with a military-pace hut-two-three-four, I made myself place two calls and each time concentrate hard on what I was saying and what was being said to me.

"You're at home, Janie?"

"Yeah, I just got in."

"All's well?"

"Oh, yeah, I'm like scared shitless. But other than that."

"You're being looked after, Tom Dunphy said."

"Some guy Anthony. He's actually kind of cute."

"So you know what happened after I left you yesterday. You must have just pulled out of the Outback. I was in the parking lot on the phone."

"I know. That is so creepy."

"I'm trying to figure out how these guys knew I was meeting with you. Did you happen to mention our four o'clock appointment to anybody yesterday?"

A silence. "I'm trying to think."

"Take your time."

After a moment she said, "Just Kev. Kev called during my break — he knows I have twelve minutes rest period from two-fifteen to two-twenty-seven — and I told him I was gonna see you at Outback and talk to you about you-know-what. But Kev wouldn't mention any of that to anybody. He respects my privacy, and he knows how I am."

"Kev is your boyfriend?"

"Yeah, Kevin LeBow. He's an installer at Verizon."

"And he supports your decision to expose Kenyon Louderbush?"

"Oh sure. Kev hates crap like that as much as I do, and also his union can't stand Louderbush."

"And there's nobody else you might have mentioned our meeting to ahead of time? What about your supervisor?"

"Oh God, no. Alma would put a letter in my file. She'd friggin' call Arkansas."

"If you were meeting with a private investigator?"

"Walmart is suspicious. But I think, like, what they don't know won't hurt them."

I thought, Kev LeBow. Could he have been recruited by the Louderbush people to ingratiate himself with Insinger and seduce her and report back on her contacts with the McCloskey campaign and its agents? Not likely. They'd been a pair for quite a while. Was I just practicing due diligence, or was I becoming as paranoid as Insinger's employer?

I told Insinger I thought she should do whatever Anthony the security guy suggested, and to be watchful otherwise, and that I'd be in touch.

I got Virgil Jackman on his cell at Jock World. He said he couldn't talk but that he had an eleven-minute break coming up and he'd call me back in ten minutes.

Timmy said, "What's a five-letter word meaning *ancient stringed instrument*? First letter *R*, third letter *B*?"

"Robot?"

"Come on."

"Rhubarb."

"The second letter might be *E*."

"Rebar."

"Not exactly a musical instrument."

"It could be. Percussion."

"Keep trying."

"I'm doing my best."

"I hope not."

Soon, Jackman called back. I asked him first how things were going with the security Tom Dunphy was providing.

"I don't really need it, but this guy Damien is okay to hang with. He follows me around in this Hummer he has. He's even bigger than I am. I'm glad he's on our side."

"It's good," I said, "that these guys went after me and not you and Janie. It means that their employer has some sense. Going after you two could generate serious backlash if you went public right away and linked Louderbush to the attacks. But by beating on me they send the message to the McCloskey campaign that they are prepared to play rough and McCloskey should have second thoughts about pursuing any exposure of Louderbush's vile behavior. Anyway, Tom Dunphy is prepared to press on, if you are. So am I."

"Sure. I'm scared, I have to admit. But I'm not gonna take any shit from somebody who did what Louderbush did to Greg. What about Janie? Is she cool?"

"It's a little bit murky as to her usefulness as a witness. But she's accepted security from the campaign, and she's still talking to us. One thing I'm doing is trying to find other people who might have witnessed the abuse or who at least had some direct knowledge of it. People Stiver confided in and who maybe saw the shiner and the split lip and the other physical damage from the beatings. There has to be somebody who knows something, even if not as much as you and Janie do."

"I got the idea," Jackman said, "that maybe Greg dropped some of his friends after he got involved with Louderbush. He was embarrassed or whatever. I know he dropped out of the gay Republicans and that other organization — upholding the Constitution and so forth. He told Janie and I he had to finish his thesis, and he didn't have time for all those people, but I'll bet it was that he didn't want anybody asking a lot of questions about his messed up appearance. I mean, how many times can you tell people you slipped in the shower or you were in a car wreck? Especially when your car wasn't banged up or anything."

"The story about his suicide in the *Times Union* said he had friends who were concerned about his being despondent. Who do you think the paper might have been referring to?"

"A reporter called Janie and I after she talked to Mrs. Pensivy. So I guess maybe that means us?"

"What about Greg's parents and his brother and sister in

Schenectady? Might he have confided in any of them?"

"He mentioned his sister, Jennifer, sometimes. She might've known something. But his mom and dad he had nothing to do with. His dad was a violent jerk and his mom was no help. I don't know about Greg's brother, Hugh. I think he moved out at some point and was no longer part of the family equation."

I made a note to track down Stiver's sister. As well as his thesis advisor.

I told Jackman that I was puzzled as to how anybody knew I was meeting him and Insinger on Wolf Road Tuesday afternoon. I asked him if he had mentioned to anyone that we planned on meeting.

"Not that I can think of," he said. "In fact, no. I was so busy at work…oh fuck! Shit! My break is over. I'm two minutes late. Shit. Gotta run, dude!"

He hung up.

I said to Timmy, "I still don't know how the Serbians knew they could find me in the Outback parking lot. Nobody involved recalls telling anybody I'd be there."

"The two Serbians and one Roma."

"Right."

"You never saw the driver of the Navigator?"

"No, just the three who jumped me."

"And you tend to believe Insinger and Jackman?"

"I tend to, yeah."

"And you trust Tom Dunphy?"

"Sure. Why not?"

"He's well thought of. Of course, the line of work he's in… well."

"You would know."

"You bet."

"No, it's not Dunphy or Jackman or Insinger who set me up,

I don't think. There's something I'm missing here."

Timmy said, "Rebec."

"What?"

"The ancient stringed instrument is a rebec."

"Never heard of it."

"Now you have."

"I would think *rebec* meant to bec again."

He ignored this and moved on. I could see that he had about three quarters of the puzzle filled in, all of it in ink.

I said, "Would you hand me the phone book, please?"

I looked up Stiver listings in Schenectady and found two: Anson on Ridgemont Drive and J Stiver on Pond Street. J for Jennifer?

I dialed the J number.

"Yes, hello?" Female, firm, clear.

"Is this Jennifer Stiver?"

The expected pause. Was I a telemarketer? "Yes, I'm Jenny. And you?"

"I'm Donald Strachey, a private investigator, and I'm calling about a matter concerning your late brother Greg. I understand from friends of Greg's that you and Greg were close."

I made out what sounded like a muttered *oh shit* before the line went dead.

CHAPTER SEVEN

Thursday morning my joints and muscles were still telling me *Don't move, just don't move at all*, and I had an enormous bruise on the side of my neck that Timmy said looked like a kind of evil hickey. The pain from my ripped ear felt as if I'd been gone after with a cheese grater, and something bad seemed to be going on with the five stitches under the bandage. My hearing was in fact impaired to a degree, but not so much that I couldn't hear Timmy's electric toothbrush buzzing in the bathroom as well as his nose-hair trimmer, his early-morning carbon footprint surprisingly sizeable for such a diehard environmentalist.

Still flat on my back, I phoned a friend at APD and asked him to e-mail me the Greg Stiver suicide police report. He said those files were on paper and he would fax the report when he got a chance later in the day.

I tried to recall who all I knew out at SUNY, preferably anybody with access to Stiver's academic and other records. No one came to mind who would have had that kind of access. Instead, I phoned a brilliantly clever IT guy I knew named Bud Giannopolous who I feared would one day end up in either the federal penitentiary or the CIA, depending on who came to appreciate his computer hacking abilities first.

"Can you get into the SUNY system?"

"Which one?"

"Student records."

"Piece of cake. But is this a grade change thing? I don't do that."

"Even for five hundred thousand dollars?"

"You jest, do you not?"

"I do. It's not that. I just want a look at the records of a guy named Gregory Stiver, a master's candidate, who killed himself in April five years ago."

"Jumped off a SUNY building, right?"

"You remember?"

"Sure. I'm acrophobic, so I always notice news stories about death by falling."

"It's not how anybody wants to go. Some of the people who jumped from the World Trade Center towers leaped in twos, holding hands. I guess that would somehow make it easier. But this Stiver jumped alone, and I can't think of anything lonelier."

"So you want his academic records?"

"Yes, including his master's thesis and who his advisor was. Plus the university's report on the suicide, as well as anything else that's in SUNY's records on Stiver. How long will this take?"

"I want to be thorough, so say an hour."

"You can e-mail me?"

"Well, yeah. Did you think I might bring it over by oxcart?"

When Timmy emerged from the bathroom, I told him I was driving over to Schenectady later in the morning to talk to any of Greg Stiver's relatives I could locate and who were willing to talk to me.

"Why don't you take a health and beauty day — both your health and your beauty have suffered — and go back to work tomorrow? The primary's not until September, and twenty-four hours won't make any serious difference."

"I'm okay. Just achy. It might be better if I keep moving."

He was getting into his perfectly laundered and pressed go-to-work duds, which had been meticulously laid out the night before. "Donald, somebody is obviously watching you, and they're going to know that you weren't scared off by the pounding they gave you on Tuesday. If the campaign is providing bodyguards for Insinger and Jackman, maybe they could also offer you a little help in that regard. Not somebody who would get in your way, but who could just tag along and serve as a deterrent. Or more than a deterrent if ever the need arose."

He waited for my response and looked as if he knew what was coming.

"Timothy, who are you talking to?"

"Yeah, I know."

"You're wasting your breath."

"Right. Macho-macho-maa-haan."

"No. It's not machismo. Alpha male strutting and posturing hold no interest for me. You know that by now, or should. I just work better alone. It's as simple as that. I need space and I need flexibility. Anyway, I'll be armed this time. I'll carry the Smith and Wesson."

He shook his head and went back to elegantly armoring himself for a day inside one of the most dysfunctional legislative bodies in the western hemisphere. "I guess I don't have to remind you of the statistics on people who carry guns around. It's nearly always the innocent that the weapons end up getting used on. With those innocent dead or maimed persons being the gun owners themselves, more often than not."

"I've avoided shooting my own pancreas out for some years now. Trust me."

"Of course I trust your judgment and your skills. But when guns start going off, luck is always an element. And you've been lucky in that regard for quite some time now."

"Timothy, remarks about my number coming up are not helpful. Jesus."

"Well, anyway it's all moot, since you stopped listening to me five minutes ago."

"No, I didn't. I'm going to be careful."

"Yes, I know you'll be careful, in your own particular way of being careful. Okay. Okay, okay."

He had his necktie on straight now, and he came over and leaned down and — holding his tie against his chest with one hand — gave me a sweet lingering Colgate kiss. Inasmuch as I had not yet brushed my teeth, it was an especially large and loving gesture.

"Careful, don't touch my ear."

"I should give it a good smack."

"Oh, you will, you will, at least figuratively speaking. But make it later in the month."

He pressed his lips against my uninjured, unbandaged ear and said into it, "Have a safe, productive day, Detective Strachey."

"That's what I aim to do, if at all possible."

§ § § §

Bud's e-mail arrived just after nine. I had dragged out of bed, showered, pulled on some jeans painfully, and made it down to the kitchen table and my laptop. Timmy had made coffee for me — his own preference was for South Asian milky sweet tea — and he left one of his favorite mugs at my place, a battered relic of his Peace Corps days in India. The mug bore the image of Ganesh, the elephant god, helper of scribes and remover of obstacles. While I ate some yogurt and a banana, I looked to see what Bud the remover of privacy walls had sent along.

Greg Stiver's undergraduate academic record was solid but otherwise unrevealing. He had been a steady B-plus, A-minus student from the beginning of his SUNY career. He did consistently well in history and the social sciences and faltered only in a freshman geology course, where he got a C.

In grad school, Stiver also did well, earning good grades and commendations from professors in economics courses ranging from statistics to "Birth Pangs of Capitalism" to "Marx Interred: Collectivism Dribbles Out." His master's thesis, called *A Trabant of an Economic System*, seemed from its introductory section to be about the collapse of the work ethic in East Germany during forty-five years of Marxist economics and political domination by the Soviet Union. I noted that Stiver's thesis adviser was a Dr. Paul Podolski. I checked the current roster of SUNY faculty; Professor Podolski was listed, and I noted his phone number, office location, and e-mail address.

The university's report on Stiver's suicide — digitalized images of typed or handwritten pages — had been compiled by campus police and was stiff with copspeak — "the subject" this, "the subject" that, and multiple references to "the deceased." No one actually witnessed Stiver's April 17 mid-morning plunge; he had jumped while classes were in session and there were no pedestrians in the immediate vicinity beside the Quad Four tower. His body was discovered adjacent to a walkway by janitorial staff on a break, apparently some minutes after Stiver had jumped. The janitors notified campus cops, who immediately called APD. The city cops responded within ten minutes and got there just before an ambulance arrived. The ambulance was pro forma; the head of the SUNY security detail had noted it was plain that Stiver's neck was broken, and his skull had cracked and brain matter had spattered across the sidewalk.

A follow-up report, dated the next day, noted that preliminarily police believed the death to be a suicide. Stiver had gained access to the roof of the building by way of an unlocked door at the top of a stairwell. His backpack with books and "personal items" was found near the spot from which he had jumped. There was no evidence anyone else had been with Stiver on the roof.

A third report, a day later, said APD reported to SUNY that detectives had been given a suicide note by the landlady of the deceased. Also, unnamed "friends" — Insinger and Jackman? — had told APD detectives that Stiver had been despondent in recent weeks. So the conclusion was that Stiver had taken his own life.

No reference was made in any of this to Stiver's sexuality or to his personal life at all, and Assemblyman Louderbush's name never came up. There was, however, a note appended to page three of the report. It read "call from Leg. Blessing responding."

Leg. was Legislature? And who or what was Blessing?

CHAPTER EIGHT

Jennifer Stiver's Facebook page contained not a lot of useful information, but I could see that she was no wounded hermit. She was pretty, open-faced, and smiling in her photo, maybe a little flirtatious, with subtly applied makeup and an unsubtle head of wild honey-colored hair. She had designated herself single. Her interests, she noted, were music, dancing, and spelunking. *Spelunking?* In her photo, Stiver had no mud on her face and she wasn't wearing a headlamp. Her birth date made her thirty-four years old. She didn't list an astrological sign, as some Facebook users did, or any other colorations of personality. Her occupation was teacher. Otherwise she was unforthcoming.

I rang Bud again.

"Strachey, you got the stuff I sent?"

"You bet. One more item before you bill me. Is there a Jennifer Stiver teaching in any of the schools, public or private, in or around Schenectady?"

"Half an hour."

"I'm here."

While I waited, I called a woman I knew at APD, and she gave me the names of the three insurance guys who saw me get beat up by the Serbians. I phoned each one in turn on their cells, and they had little to add to what Hanratty had told me. They all apologized for not getting the tag number of the Lincoln, and they all said they were surprised I was out of the hospital so soon. They said I looked terrible lying there in my own blood, and at first they weren't sure I wasn't dead. One of the three, a man named Servan Singh, said he noticed that the Navigator had a green sticker on a rear side window that looked like some kind of landfill permit. I wondered, for dumping trash or bodies?

Bud called me back. "Jennifer Stiver teaches sixth grade at Burton Hendricks Elementary School in Rotterdam. She's been there for eight years. Her personnel file contains excellent evaluations overall. Should I send them along?"

"No, no need."

"There was one negative thing five years ago, not coincidentally I suppose, around the time of her brother's death. Her principal notes that she missed two weeks of school, which was a week longer than the bereavement policy allowed. She was docked a week's pay and warned not to miss any more days that were unauthorized."

"I wonder why she didn't just say she was sick that second week. She must have had sick leave accumulated."

"Maybe she recognized that that would have been dishonest."

"I'm glad to have you of all people point that out to me, Bud."

"Thinking you might need to know, I also learned that Ms. Stiver is now winding up her teaching duties for the school year. The last day of classes at Burton Hendricks is a week from tomorrow."

"What time does school let out today? Surely you looked into that also."

"Three-fifteen."

Bud gave me the address for the school, and I asked him to stand by and not leave town. I said I was working on something both fascinating and disturbing, and he would learn about it soon enough and it would leave him disgusted.

"Cool."

I finished getting clothes on and took another Tylenol. I still ached all over and my ripped ear was throbbing. I retrieved and loaded the Smith & Wesson. The Weather Channel called for a high of eighty-three, so there was no way I was going to wear anything that would conceal the weapon. I stuck it in the black shoulder bag I carried when traveling in Europe and Asia. The gun nestled in there nicely with my map of Istanbul and my Imodium.

I phoned the SUNY economics department. A secretary said Dr. Paul Podolski might be able to see me after his two-hour nine o'clock summer-school class. SUNY was on the way to Rotterdam, more or less, so I went out and was about to climb into the Toyota when I thought, oh shit, car bomb.

With effort, I got down and checked the wheel wells — nothing amiss — and then popped the hood and examined the engine. Nothing wrong there either, other than some corroded battery terminals. I thought, this is nuts. What the hell am I thinking? The Serbians warned me to get off the Louderbush investigation, and they don't even know that I'm still on it, so why would they try to blow me up? Several people — two of them other Crow Street denizens I knew vaguely — strolled by while I was inspecting the car. None seemed to be watching me or showing any interest at all in what I was doing.

I got in and turned the key and was not blown to bits. I pulled out onto Crow, then turned up Hudson. I checked the rearview mirror periodically and headed out Lark and then left on Washington Avenue toward the SUNY main campus. Some fair-weather clouds drifted across a pale early summer sky, and I opened the car windows and sucked in air that felt unusually clean and fresh. I thought, I hurt but I am inhaling and exhaling like a pro. *Nice.*

The State University of New York Albany main campus — which cost hundreds of millions of dollars when it was strewn across a field by Nelson Rockefeller in the 1960s but by now looked only a little more alluring than a hot-sheet motel in Fort Lee — was sparsely populated during its summer semihiatus, and those few students and others out and about were in no big hurry. I parked and soon located Quad Four, the classroom tower from which Greg Stiver had plunged to his death. I thought I figured out the spot where he had landed. There were no aftereffects, no memorial plaque. I paused for a minute, then moved on.

Paul Podolski had a third-floor office in a nearby building, another cement and glass upended shoe box, the public architecture of a society wary of overspending in an area it was ambivalent about, such as learning.

I was told by the department secretary to knock on the door of room 318, but when I found 318 the door was open and a man looked up from a computer terminal.

"Yep? What's up?"

He looked like one of the Smith Brothers on the cough drop box, skinny, shiny on top and black beard from upper lip to midsection I introduced myself and said I understood he had been Gregory Stiver's thesis adviser, and I asked if I might talk to him about Greg for a few minutes.

"Maybe. Who are you working for, may I ask?"

"I can't really say who my client is at this point. But I can tell you it's somebody entirely sympathetic to Greg, someone who is very sorry about Greg's death and the circumstances leading up to it."

He sat there sizing me up. Who was I, and what was I up to? "What circumstances are you referring to? What circumstances leading up to Greg's suicide? That is, if it was suicide."

I helped myself to a seat in the chair across Podolski's desk from him. "I'm talking about Greg's unhappiness in the weeks before he died. The police and press reports both refer to Greg's supposed despondency. What do you mean, if it was suicide? You have doubts?"

"All I'm saying is, I didn't expect Greg to do such a thing. It was shocking to me."

"He hadn't been depressed that you were aware of? Two friends say he was. Janie Insinger and Virgil Jackman were neighbors of Greg's and rode with him from his place on Allen Street out here to the campus a couple of times a week."

"It's true," Podolski said, "that I didn't see as much of Greg after his thesis was accepted as I did in the previous months. Which I was actually sorry about. I always enjoyed talking with Greg. He was quite bright, and I always thought somebody that smart could be led away from his rather simplistic ideas about the vaunted glories of laissez faire capitalism. And he loved to explain to me how my supposedly socialist ideas — I'm actually a kind of Jack Kennedy accomodationist Democrat — were a form of the very tyranny the founders of the republic had rebelled against.

"Greg and I spent a lot of time poking and jabbing at each other on these matters, without either of us ever giving an inch. But we respected each other, and Greg's thesis on the half-century erosion of the work ethic in the German Democratic Republic was a well-written and nicely argued piece of work. I had encouraged Greg to turn the thesis into an article for, say, the *National Review* — I know an editor there — and he seemed quite eager to do that. I know he had just about finished a draft when he died, and he was planning on showing it to me. So, really, I was just stunned when he fell off Quad Four and was killed, and pretty soon out came an official verdict of suicide, of all things."

Was this the Greg Stiver Insinger and Jackman had described to me? Could there somehow be two Greg Stivers? I said, "Wasn't he anxious about getting a teaching job? His friends said he was, and he'd been turned down by two colleges."

"I think there were a couple of things that didn't pan out, yes, but one of those institutions — someplace out near Rochester — Hall Creek Community College, I think I recall — had a spot that opened up unexpectedly. Greg knew somebody out there who tipped him off to the opening and was lobbying for him. So the job situation wasn't all that bleak, in my estimation. And then suddenly Greg died. It was appalling, really. One of those deaths that, when it happens, is just incomprehensible."

"Did you attend the funeral?"

"I did. It was depressing too. No acknowledgement of the absurdity of Greg's death at all. But then I do understand that that isn't what funerals are for. For absurdity we go to Beckett or Sartre, not Calvin."

"Who attended the funeral? Did you know the people there?"

Podolski fidgeted. "You know, I'm really curious about who is asking questions about Greg's death five years after it happened. So does this mean that someone besides me is suspicious of the suicide verdict?"

"Yes, someone is," I said, and I wasn't lying because I knew as soon as I said it that I meant myself. "There's no evidence of foul play. At this point it just has to do with someone Greg was involved with. May I ask what you knew about his personal life?"

"Not much. I knew Greg was gay. He was active with the Log Cabin Republicans. Or had been. I know during his second year in the graduate program he cut back on most of the extracurricular stuff so he could concentrate on course work and on his thesis. And of course on playing rugby supposedly."

"Greg played rugby? This is the first I've heard that."

"That's what he told me. Though I sometimes wondered. He'd come to see me all banged up — bruised, a split lip, a shiner one time. It happened every so often, and he'd shrug it off and say rugby was just something he needed to do to burn off tension. But I have to say, I knew a few other rugby players, and none of them ever looked like they'd been run over by a truck the way Greg did. And this seemed to happen regularly. It occurred to me he might be — let me just put it bluntly — in an abusive relationship."

"You never asked him?"

"Once I did, actually. I thought I had to. I said something about his black eye, and had somebody socked him one? This was a chance for him to open up if he wanted to. But he didn't pick up on this. He said oh, no, it was just a wicked weekend game with some of the rougher players in his league. I let it go after that, thinking that either he had to work this out on his own at his own pace, or that maybe I was just imagining the whole thing as to any abuse. Educators used to be inattentive about this sort of thing, and now maybe we've overcompensated and we've gotten hypersensitive. It's hard these days to know when to butt in and when to butt out."

"Any signs of a rugby team at Greg's funeral?"

"Not that I noticed. It seemed to be mainly family and friends of the Stiver family, plus a few other faculty and students from the econ department. There was somebody from the Federalist Society I recognized."

"Both of Greg's parents were there?"

"I believe so. Why wouldn't they be?"

"I've been told Greg's father, Anson, is a nasty piece of work, and they didn't get along."

"I didn't know that, but then Greg never talked about his family at all with me. He preferred to talk economic theory and history, and it was the nature of our relationship that he could do that with me and just lose himself in it, the way some people lose themselves in drugs or sports memorabilia or line dancing. I'm a little bit that way myself with economic theory, although I do manage to have a life otherwise. My wife sees to it that I come out of my academic cave from time to time, and I am grateful to her for that."

"What about political figures? Were there any at the funeral?"

Podolski tugged at his beard as if to stimulate memory. "None that I'm aware of. Why do you ask? Is your investigation politically related somehow?"

"Possibly. It's too soon to tell what my investigation is really about or where it might lead."

"Does somebody think Greg might have been pushed off Quad Four? I have to say, I've been haunted by that possibility ever since he died. I assumed at the time that the police would have considered foul play, and then they rejected it based on the evidence they had. Of course, if they had asked my opinion about Greg committing suicide, I'd have told them that to me it was unlikely. But they never asked. Apparently they based their conclusion on the physical evidence and little else."

"The Albany cops did talk to Greg's neighbors, Janie Insinger and Virgil Jackman, who told them that Greg had been anxious and depressed for many weeks. Did Greg ever mention Insinger and Jackman to you?"

"Not that I recall."

"Those two also told me that Greg was romantically involved with a political figure he met when this man visited one of Greg's classes at SUNY. Do you know who they might have been referring to?"

More beard tugging. "None comes to mind. Political figure? On rare occasions members of the State Legislature are on campus for one reason or another. Or the governor. Who was governor five years ago? George Pataki, I guess. Or — I have to ask — do you actually know who the politician was that Greg was getting it on with and you're just being coy with me?"

"I'm trying to be discreet. Call it coy if you want to."

"Then I suppose I could figure it out. I could ask around the department. But why don't you just tell me who it was and save me a lot time?"

"Kenyon Louderbush."

"The Tea Party guy running for governor?"

"Yes."

"Yuck."

"Republicans can be sexy. I've read that one reason Laura Bush has stuck with her doofus of a husband for so many years is, she considers him a hot number."

"That's enough about Laura and W behind closed doors. As my students sometimes say, TMI."

"Couldn't Louderbush have visited a class without your knowledge?"

"Possible but not likely. I'm vice chair of the department, and faculty always give me or Doris Carpenter, who's the chair, a heads-up as to any visiting royalty. Legislators have to be wined and dined, at least figuratively speaking. And Louderbush is one of those budget-committee characters whose presence in the department — or on campus at all — would be taken very, very seriously by the powers that be around here. No, I would have known about Louderbush showing up on campus. I really doubt that that's where the two of them met."

This was getting confusing. I said, "I keep getting different stories from different people as to who Greg Stiver was and how he led his life and what his state of mind was in the months before he died. He was depressed, he wasn't depressed. He was an isolated economics wonk in an abusive relationship, or he was an eager young man looking forward to launching a career in academia who let off steam regularly by charging around and getting banged up on a rugby field. Greg's story gets more *Rashomon*like by the hour."

Podolski seemed to be gazing at my bandaged ear. "It looks like you're into rugby pretty heavily yourself, Donald. Or is your own story also more complicated than you're letting on?"

"You could say so, yeah."

"Anyway, I love your bag."

CHAPTER NINE

Loitering in a car outside an elementary school is a good way to draw unwanted attention if you're not the parent of one or more of the pupils inside. So I parked in what appeared to be the staff lot, locked the shoulder bag in the trunk of the Corolla, and strode up to the uniformed security guard outside the main entrance. The stout, seventyish, Caucasian man was shifting this way and that, looking as if he was about ready to finish his shift and get the heck off school property and go somewhere and have a smoke — I could smell it on him — and a brew. The curb fifty feet away was lined with idling school buses, their drivers poised, awaiting the onslaught.

"Sir, I'm looking for Jennifer Stiver. Is she likely to come out this way?"

"Prob'ly."

"So, school's out in three minutes?"

"Yeah, about that. But the teachers won't be out yet. They mostly stay late."

"Will Jenny be in her classroom?"

"Prob'ly."

"I'm her cousin Donald from Minneapolis. She doesn't even know I'm in town. Aunt Elva thought I should surprise Jenny and she'd get a kick out of that."

"That's nice. She's in room twenty-six. Just tell the office first."

"Thank you, sir."

I stood aside when a bell went off, the entire building seemed to tremble on its foundations, and the doors burst open and unleashed a hopping and skipping swarm of small people jabbering and hollering. The loading of the buses by the drivers and cadres of aides was carried out as efficiently as any UPS overnight sorting operation. None of the hundreds of first-to-sixth graders wandered off or fell under a bus or sneaked behind a bush to smoke pot. Within a fast five minutes, the buses shut their doors and roared down the street in a mighty convoy behind which lesser traffic would soon creep along, in Buddhist-monk-like synchronicity with a universe that was orderly and moral twice a day.

I nodded at the security guy and ambled inside the building, a one-story concrete slab and glass structure with classroom wings extending out from the administrative core and, presumably, a cafeteria and gym in the rear. I waltzed past the office — a sign said OFFICE — and turned down a corridor, hoping this was the wing with room 26.

It was. The door was open, and I peered inside. My idea was, if I approached Jennifer Stiver in any number of other situations, she would likely tell me to buzz off, or even run away. If I approached her in her workplace, she might possibly do either of those, but she might also be such a slave to professional decorum that she'd be willing to talk to me.

"Ms. Stiver?"

"Yes?" She looked uncertain. Was I a parent or stepparent or other family member of a student who she wasn't quite remembering?

"I'm sorry to bother you in your classroom. I'm sure you're up to here with end-of-the-school-year responsibilities. But I know how close you were to your brother Greg, and I'm sure you were devastated by his suicide. I'm Donald Strachey, a private investigator, and I've been hired by other people who cared about Greg to look into the circumstances of Greg's death, and I'm hoping you'll be able to clear up some inconsistencies I've run into about Greg's state of mind in the weeks prior to his death."

She stood next to her desk glaring at me. She was taller than she looked in her Facebook photo, her amber hair was even more meticulously unruly, and her big china-blue eyes were bright with anger.

"You're working for people who *cared* about Greg? And who

exactly would those people be who supposedly cared about Greg? I think you're a fucking liar is what I think you are. Did you by chance call me last night at home?"

"I did. You hung up on me. Can you say *fucking* in an elementary school? I'm surprised."

"Well, your shock would disappear in a hurry if you spent a day with today's sixth graders."

"Do you wash their mouths out with soap, or how do you handle present-day potty mouthery?"

"No, I do not wash their mouths out with soap, nor do I touch the children in any way whatsoever that could be construed as corporal punishment. What I do is, I explain, without actually saying it, that *fuck* is a rude word, and life is nicer for everybody if we refrain from using rude words in the same way we should all try to refrain from using rude behavior. Sometimes this argument makes an impression, although often it doesn't. Back when I was a naive beginning teacher I once asked a boy if he used language like that in front of his parents. He said yeah, he did, and if they didn't like the way he talked, they could go fuck themselves."

"Gee. And you're not allowed to Taser the children?"

"No. Even though electronic zapping would not involve touching a child, it's not permitted. But I am allowed to Taser uninvited classroom intruders such as yourself, or at least to call security. First, though, let me ask you something. Are you by chance working for a life insurance company?"

"No, why?"

She relaxed a little now and looked not so much outraged as merely nettled. "Well, who *are* you working for, and what's your interest in Greg's death? Greg died more than five years ago. His insurance company, Shenango Life, not only refused to pay out benefits but seemed to be hinting that I had something to do with Greg's suicide. I was the intended beneficiary of his fifty-thousand-dollar policy, and they acted as if I was an accomplice in an attempt to defraud the company. When you called last night, I thought, oh God, it's Shenago Life driving me up the wall all over again."

"I'm not surprised," I said, "that you were Greg's life insurance beneficiary. Greg's relationship with his boyfriend — if that's the correct term for his friendship with Kenyon Louderbush — was apparently troubled. I guess he wasn't about to leave that violently unstable guy fifty thousand dollars."

I didn't know what the cold look she gave me meant, but she abruptly walked over and shut the door to the classroom.

"Okay, sit down."

"Thank you."

"If Mrs. Weaver, the principal, drops in, I'll say you're a friend."

"I told the security guy I was your cousin from Minneapolis."

"Fine. Cousin Donald. Just so no one thinks you're a guy I'm dating. If word went around that I was dating an aging kickboxer, I'd be really embarrassed."

"No kickboxing for me, not to worry. If it's my banged-up appearance you're referring to, it's only rugby. My boyfriend thinks I'm getting a little old for that stuff, but I can't seem to give it up."

This fib had the approximate intended effect. "You're gay. Okay. Now I'm supposed to see you as less threatening than I did two minutes ago. All right, I do. So, did you actually know Greg?"

She was perched on the edge of her desk now, and I eased onto one of the sixth graders' chairs in the front row. Stiver needed to feel as if she was in charge of the situation, and that was fine with me because in all the most important ways she was.

"No," I said, "I didn't know Greg at all. I'm just learning about him. I've met his neighbors on Allen Street, Janie Insinger and Virgil Jackman, and I've met his thesis adviser, Professor Podolski. They all spoke well of Greg and were very sad when he died. The thing is, someone has hired me to look more closely at Greg's relationship with someone else who was very important in his life: Kenyon Louderbush. You knew about that, I take it."

A tight look. "Of course."

"And you were aware that it was abusive? That Louderbush beat Greg?"

"Yes." She shook her head and looked as if she might cry. She walked around and plopped onto the chair behind her desk. "Look, here's the thing if you really have to know. I tried to get Greg into therapy so he could put an end to this horrible, masochistic self-destructiveness. But he wouldn't do it. He said he had to finish his thesis, and that was the only thing he had the energy for. Then when the thesis was done, it was some other reason. He was going to be moving away from Albany, and he said there was no point in starting therapy around here and then quitting, and he would do it after he got settled wherever he ended up. My hope, of course, was that he'd move somewhere far away from Kenyon, and he'd be okay at least until he found someone else who would treat him the way he thought he deserved to be treated. That is, really, really badly."

"That had to do with his father? Insinger and Jackman both said Greg had been beaten as a child by his father. Your father."

"Our stepfather actually, Anson Stiver. Our dad, Jim Cutler, died in a car accident when Greg and Hugh and I were one, four and six, and Mom married Anson the next year and he insisted that we all change our last names. I'm glad," she said, nodding approvingly, "that Greg was able to talk to someone else about how Anson beat him and Hugh almost from the day he moved in. Greg told me he'd opened up about it to a few people, but I never knew who they were. Kenyon, of course, knew. But to him, that knowledge just gave him the means to exploit Greg in his sick way."

"So Hugh was also abused? But not you?"

"I have no idea why I was spared. Maybe because Mom and I were close when I was young, and I was a girl, and Mom wouldn't have put up with Anson hurting me. But she looked the other way when Anson beat Greg and Hugh. I think she saw it as the price the family was going to have to pay for financial security. Well, it was way, way too high a price. Hugh was so traumatized by his upbringing that he left Schenectady as soon as he turned eighteen, and he hasn't been in touch with any of us since then. Greg actually grew up to be a sane and functioning adult and one of the nicest people I've ever known. Of course he was so fucked up by the abuse from Anson that he must have thought at some level that for him intimacy could only be violent. It all just makes me so really, really mad."

"You know, of course, that Louderbush is now running for governor in the Democratic primary."

"Oh yes. I know that. Who doesn't? And it occurs to me that that's the reason you're here. Am I right, Donald?"

"You are. Kenyon Louderbush is not morally fit for the governorship. He's not fit for the State Assembly either, but if all the assemblymen unfit to serve suddenly vacated the Capitol, it would be a thinly populated institution."

She gave me an I-should-have-seen-this-coming look. "So, which side are you digging up dirt for? McCloskey, I'll bet."

"Does that matter? What counts is that Louderbush is forced out of the race and never gets to be governor."

"You know, after Greg died I almost went to the police about Kenyon. I truly believed that Greg's death was legally a form of manslaughter. That Kenyon had somehow driven Greg to take his own life. But I was so upset over the whole depressing mess that I was just paralyzed for a while. I stayed out of school for two terrible weeks and barely got out of bed. The only reason I eventually got my act together was, I was terrified I'd be fired. And with all my student loans I just couldn't afford to lose my job here. Also, I missed my kids. So I came back to school and just concentrated on saving my teaching career. And time went by, and I got distracted by one thing or another, and I never did turn Kenyon in. But I felt I had to do *something*. So instead I wrote Kenyon a letter."

"What did you say in the letter?"

"I told him he was cruel and heartless and psychologically disturbed, and that I blamed him for Greg's death, and I knew that someday his bad karma would catch up with him and he would pay for all the suffering and pain he had caused."

"You sent this letter to Louderbush's office?"

"Yes, I did. I didn't care who saw it."

"Did he reply?"

She shook her head and laughed once. "Well, I think he did."

"What do you mean?"

"It wasn't until about a month later that I received a plain envelope at my apartment mailbox with no return address. Inside the envelope was a one-page letter that had been typed on a word processor and wasn't signed. The writer was careful not to reveal anything about his identity, but it was obviously from Kenyon. He said I didn't understand his relationship with Greg, and if I did I would not be so judgmental. He said he and Greg had loved and needed each other, and they had been planning to find a way to control their own worst impulses — that was the term he used — and make a life together. I thought, a life together? The man was delusional. He was married with children and was a family-values conservative in the Legislature. He might have convinced Greg that they had some kind of future, and he might even have believed it himself at some level. But I thought it was a sick joke."

"Did you tell him that?"

"No. I was thoroughly disgusted, and I just decided to move on. I have to say, I rarely thought of Kenyon until I saw that he was running for governor. That's when it all came flooding back — Greg and Kenyon and the violence and the suicide — and I was sick in my soul all over again. I thought, I can't let this go. I *have* to do something. So I called the Republicans and told them about Greg and about Kenyon."

"You called the Ostwind campaign? When was this?"

"Back in January, right after New Year's. It never occurred to me that they wouldn't take me seriously, but that's exactly what happened. A woman called me — Meg-something — and she said it wasn't right for the campaign to be prying into their opponents' personal lives. She asked me what proof I had of an abusive relationship. I said I believed what Greg had told me, but on top of that I only had the typed letter from Kenyon that wasn't signed and could have been written by anybody. When I told her this, she said I had better forget the whole thing. She said it was hearsay. That was her word: hearsay."

"Legally, that's true. But you weren't initiating a legal proceeding."

"No, I was trying to stop a total asshole from becoming governor of New York."

"That's exactly what I'm trying to do."

"It really upset me that the Ostwind people didn't get what I was saying. I mean, I'm a Republican and I want Merle Ostwind to win. I was trying to *help*, for fuck's sake."

"Yes, you were."

"Well, anyway, I guess this proves that you aren't working for the Ostwind campaign. You don't represent some belated attempt to take my information seriously."

"No, that's not what I'm doing here."

Now she looked even more troubled. "So I guess that means you are working for Shy McCloskey. You're trying to get the goods on Kenyon and hurt him politically."

"You could draw that conclusion, Jennifer. By a process of elimination."

She shook her head. "Oh crap. This puts me in a real bind. Of course I want to stop Kenyon from getting elected. But I don't really know how helpful I can be to you, because I certainly don't want to see Shy McCloskey win the election. He's *way* too liberal. McCloskey is in the pocket of the unions. That includes the AFT, which protects lazy, ineffective teachers who should have been canned years ago but are still ruining children's lives because liberals like Shy McCloskey are too cowardly to face reality and are too beholden financially to the unions. Greg explained to me years ago how all that worked, and since then I've added to my knowledge of liberalism's failures with what I've seen with my own eyes."

This was not what I had tracked Jennifer Stiver down to hear her say. "But don't you think Greg would want Kenyon Louderbush stopped from being elected governor?"

She got teary-eyed again and sniffled. "Yes. Yes and no. No and yes. I know Greg was very, very hurt by his masochistic relationship with Kenyon. But would he have wanted Kenyon to become governor of New York? In all honesty, I'd have to say I'm not really sure he wouldn't have."

Chapter Ten

All four tires on the Toyota had been slashed. There was no other damage to the car. What was done would have been carried out discreetly, what with teachers and other staff moving about in the school parking lot while I was inside being both helped and hindered by Jennifer Stiver.

I knew that the tire job had been done by the Serbians — and not by sixth-graders who go around saying fuck — because a handwritten note had been stuck under my windshield wiper. It read *This is your second and final warning.*

Okay, so they had followed me? I was certainly unaware of any tail when I left the house in the morning and when I was cruising around the all-but-deserted SUNY parking lot next to Paul Podolski's office building. I'd stopped for lunch at the Gateway diner on Central Avenue, and I guessed they might have spotted me there and followed me to Rotterdam. But were they staking out all the upper Hudson Valley lunch spots in case I got hungry? Hardly. Who had I told that I was seeing Podolski and then Jennifer Stiver? Timmy and…Bud? Bud was on the good guy's side, I was certain, or at least on the team that was paying his fat fee. Computer hackers operated outside the law, but they had their own rigid code of ethics, like *Good Housekeeping* and the Tupac Amaru.

I looked at the note again. This was my second and final warning, but my final warning before what?

I phoned a Triple A garage in Schenectady, explained that my tires had been vandalized and I would need a car carrier, not just a tow, and also a lift and a rental car. They said forty-five minutes.

One by one, two women and two men walked out of the school while I waited, took note of my flat tires, and asked me what had happened. I said, "My ex-girlfriend is pissed off. I suppose she has her reasons." Each of these people peered at my car and at my bandaged ear and at my giant hickey, and then nodded, walked on and drove away.

Jennifer Stiver soon appeared, but she was busy talking on her cell phone and got into a red Dodge Neon parked nearer the school building and drove off without noticing me.

I phoned Timmy at work and explained my situation, leaving out the part about the final warning note.

"Oh, good grief. Do you want me to come out and pick you up?"

"No need. I'll get a rental car. Anyhow, it might be good to have an anonymous car for a day or two. I'm also thinking of staying in a hotel overnight. I can't figure out how these people seem to know where I am all the time."

"Could they have hidden an electronic tracker somewhere in your car?"

"This is looming as a possibility. I've checked the car for explosives but not for a tracker. After I get the car back, I'll ask the campaign's security people to take a look. Dunphy uses Clean-Tech, and I know they're good. If there's anything to be found, they'll find it. Meanwhile, I should be as elusive as possible for a while."

"You actually checked the car for explosives? I thought you said these people weren't trying to kill you, just to warn you off."

"That's true. I'm just being overdramatic. Anyway, they somehow seem to know that I'm still working on getting the goods on Kenyon Louderbush, and they badly want me to stop. This only confirms that Louderbush is a despicable human being who must never be elected governor."

"Any idea yet who *they* are? I assume it's the actual Louderbush campaign."

"Maybe. Though it could be out-of-control Tea Partiers or other right-wing fringe types who are doing bad things on Louderbush's behalf without him or his campaign people knowing exactly what's going on. So if anything leaks out Louderbush will have plausible deniability."

"It sounds like the Nixon White House."

"You don't have to go that far back. Don't forget Cheney and Rove and the Valerie Plame CIA outing. I doubt Bush himself ever knew."

"Was Jennifer Stiver helpful at all? What was she like?"

"She was helpful in the sense that she confirmed that her brother was a tortured soul who had been taken advantage of by a sadistic creep. And she doesn't seem to doubt that Greg took his own life. She was unhelpful in the sense that, like her brother, she's a conservative Republican and she wants Merle Ostwind to win the governor's race, and she's unwilling to do anything that might get Shy McCloskey elected. Ms. Stiver doesn't like liberals."

"You didn't wave your ACLU card in her face, I take it."

"I didn't need to. I'm working for the McCloskey campaign, and that's bad enough. I tried to leave the impression that I'm merely mercenary, figuring that as a good Republican she would approve of that. But now she apparently just thinks of me as unprincipled. So I don't know how much use Jennifer's going to be in exposing Louderbush."

"What a rat's nest you've stepped in. Any second thoughts about getting involved in this?"

"No. The one thing that's clear to me is, Louderbush is a rat who has to be kept out of the governor's mansion. Anything else that's ambiguous here pales in comparison to the importance of driving Louderbush out of the race for governor."

"Are you convinced that Louderbush actually drove Greg Stiver to kill himself, as his neighbors think happened?"

"Yes and no. No and yes. I have no clear idea what happened. And neither, really, does anybody else that I've talked to so far. But I'm a long way from finished. It looks, in fact, as if I'm just getting started. Anyway, the primary is still three months away."

"I thought Dunphy wanted answers next Tuesday at the latest, and last Tuesday would be even better."

"Yes, but he also wants me to get this right. The worst thing that could happen to McCloskey is if we're somehow all wrong about Louderbush and his relationship with Greg Stiver, and the whole reeking mess suddenly blows up in McCloskey's face. That could create a big sympathy vote for Louderbush, and then both McCloskey and Ostwind would be screwed."

"That borders on plausible."

"I'm not sure I'll be home for dinner. I may go lie down somewhere. I'm still sore all over and the ear is still throbbing. Should it still be doing that?"

"I think so. Body parts that have been partially detached are going to hurt for a while. I do wish, Don, that you could just let this thing go at least for a few days while you heal. Really."

"I won't be doing anything too strenuous, not to worry. There are a few more people I need to talk to, and I'm guessing those contacts will lead to others and with luck a clearer picture will emerge. Or it won't emerge, and then the hell with our pals the Democrats."

"All that will be just as true two or three days from now when you're not feeling so wounded and drained."

"Noted."

He knew when he had made his point with me and I had considered it and I was jolly well going to do as I jolly well pleased. He recited an obscure Buddhist good-luck mantra he had picked up on our trip to Thailand a few years earlier. Then he called me a few names in Sanskrit and rang off.

Triple A hadn't shown up yet, so I called Bud Giannopolous.

"Can you get into a life insurance company's policyholder records?"

"Sure."

"Greg Stiver had a fifty-thousand-dollar policy that Shenango Life apparently weaseled out of honoring. Stiver's sister Jennifer was to have been the beneficiary. I need to know if in fact it really happened that way. And I need to know if Shenengo's investigator concurred with the police finding of suicide, or if he or she had any other ideas, and if so what they were. And of course I'd like to know whether or not Kenyon Louderbush figured anywhere in the company's report."

"Okay."

"You'll call me?"

"Later tonight."

I retrieved the bag with the Smith & Wesson from the trunk of my disabled car and stretched out on the grass while a few stragglers made their way out of the elementary school and into their cars and out onto the street. I studied the warning note left by the Serbians. It had been hand-lettered with a felt pen on a piece of ordinary copying paper. Fingerprints? In case the FBI was later involved in the case, pending my gangland-related demise, I placed the note under the front passenger seat of the car, taking care to handle it only by its edges.

The Triple A guy was bug-eyed at the sight of my car with its four flats.

"Who did it?"

"My ex-girlfriend, I think."

"Holy shit. Did you call the cops?"

"No, that would really set her off. I just have to face the fact that the relationship is over."

The guy used a winch to drag the car up a ramp onto his flatbed truck.

I said, "Won't this hurt the wheels?"

"It might."

I got to sit high up next to the driver for the ride into Schenectady.

"It looks like your ex-girlfriend went to work on you, too," the Triple A guy said.

"You noticed."

"You must be glad to be rid of her."

"Tell me about it."

I picked up a Hyundai at the rental agency across the street from the garage. My car would be ready to drive in the morning, but I told the garage, "Just hang onto it."

I needed my laptop, so I drove into Albany and found a parking spot on Dove Street only a block from the house. Timmy was not yet home from work. I checked the fax machine, and there was the five-page police report on Greg Stiver's death my friend at APD had promised to send me. I folded it and stuffed it into the shoulder bag with my gun. I packed an overnight bag and left with it, the shoulder bag, and my laptop.

I went out the back door, down the steps, across our tiny urban patch of scraggly lawn, and up onto the wooden crate that had housed some statuary we had had shipped back from Thailand. I climbed over the fence into the backyard that abutted Timmy's and mine. I knocked on the kitchen door of Dot and Edith, a lesbian couple I had helped out some years earlier when they lived on a farm and who were now quite old. Dot led me through the house and out her front door. She was used to this; I'd done it a number of times.

The rental car was as I'd left it. There seemed to be no need to check it for explosives. Though when I turned the key in the ignition, I held my breath for just an instant, and I could feel my heart thudding.

CHAPTER ELEVEN

I phoned Tom Dunphy and told him I was staying at the Crowne Plaza and that if he looked out his office window up State Street he might see me waving at him from mine.

"The Super 8 was fully booked? What are you doing putting up at the Crowne Plaza on the campaign's meager dime? Christ Almighty."

"This place is convenient to your office. Basically I'm hiding out. Those assholes slashed my tires, and they warned me again to back off." I described my visits with Paul Podolski and Jennifer Stiver and then the vandalism.

"How the hell do they know where you are all the time? I don't get that."

"I don't either. I would like my car checked for a tracking device or for listening devices as soon as I get it back, probably tomorrow. I'm driving a rental car that's parked in the hotel garage. If they track me here, I'm going to be very weirded out."

"So Stiver's sister isn't going to be much help exposing Louderbush? That's a shame."

"She actually seems to think her brother might have wanted Louderbush to become governor."

"That's sick."

"Or something. It does complicate our strategy here. Of course, we don't know what Greg Stiver would have wanted. To the extent that he confided in anybody at all, he seemed to leave different impressions with different people and even to tell entirely different stories."

"But it sounds as if you're making headway. Building a narrative."

"A narrative? Yeah, if you consider *Naked Lunch* a narrative. This is just a lot of ugly confusion and atmospherics and impressions."

"Anyway, I'll tell Shy you're on top of this, or soon will be. Don, I've heard so much about you and I know we can count on you."

I'd had enough of Dunphy for one day and rang off and called Timmy.

"Are you at home?"

"Yes. Where are you?"

"In room 612 at the Crowne Plaza. Not to worry. Nobody knows I'm here, and I'm resting and popping Tylenol."

"You can get room service and then a good night's sleep. Would you like me to come over?"

"Thanks, but there's no need. I'll be going over the police report on the suicide, and later I'll be getting briefed on the insurance investigator's report on Stiver's death. And then I'm sure I'll lapse happily into unconsciousness."

"The insurance company is letting you see their report? Those companies are so protective of that sort of thing. How did you manage to get hold of it?"

"I don't have it yet. I found somebody who has access."

"Wow, who?"

"A guy I know."

"What? Why are you being so cagey? Is this some guy you used to sleep with? Who is it?"

"No, I barely know the guy. It's just somebody who does research for me once in a while."

"Oh, a leg man."

"Yeah, leg man. Not an ass man, ha ha."

"Ha ha. Is it Bud Giannopolous?"

"Yes. Yes, it is Bud Giannopolous."

A silence. "Bud is eventually going to go to prison, you know. Do you want to go with him?"

"I should never have told you about Bud. You take this kind of thing way too seriously. It's the world we live in, Timothy."

"Yes, it's the world *we* live in. We being the Russian mafia, the Pakistani intelligence services, the North Korean Politburo, al Qaeda, and Dick Cheney. The rest of us *we*'s still respect the institutional and personal privacy that's one of the cornerstones of what's left of civilization. What Bud does is immoral, and it is illegal."

"But not fattening?"

"This is not funny. You are going to end up in the federal pen. And when it happens you'll — it hurts me to say this — you'll deserve it." He muttered something else and hung up.

God. al Qaeda? He'd never called me that one before.

I phoned room service and ordered gazpacho, a Caesar salad, and a Sam Adams.

The police report on Greg Stiver's death was a chore to wade through. How could anybody with a five-hundred word vocabulary be this verbose? The document basically repeated in its stiff, dense way what the SUNY cops had said: the body discovered at ten twenty in the morning; the apparent plunge from the Quad Four roof; death as a result of brain and other injuries. A Detective Ivor Nichols had interviewed Mrs. Pensivy, Stiver's landlady, along with Janie Insinger and Virgil Jackman, and the two "friends of the deceased" had spoken of his having been depressed over employment and other difficulties. They apparently had not mentioned Kenyon Louderbush and all that *mishegoss*. Why? Nor was there any reference to "call from Leg. Blessing responding," as in the handwritten note on the SUNY report on the incident. The presumed suicide note was quoted — "I hurt too much" — but there was no photo of the note itself and no mention of what had become of it.

I read the report a second time, and then a third, and then the soup, salad, and beer arrived. With the safety lock on the door in place, I retrieved the Smith & Wesson from my shoulder bag and placed it next to my laptop. Why had I taken it out? Roaches?

Bedbugs? I did believe I was safe in this room, whose number was known only to Timmy and to the hotel front desk.

Down below on State Street the last office-worker stragglers were heading out of the neighborhood, which would soon be all but deserted. Albany nightlife, such as it was on a Thursday evening in June, would take place largely on the outskirts of the city. Only a few hardcore pols and the lobbyists that kept the officeholders' throats hydrated and their arteries clogged would be hanging around downtown at the few ancient joints like Jack's Oyster House that somehow had survived the long-ago retail and entertainment flight to the suburbs.

While I ate, I did an Internet search for Hugh Stiver, Greg's brother, who, according to Jennifer, had lit out for parts unknown at the earliest opportunity. I found a total of nineteen Hugh Stivers, but none seemed to be the right age or race or — for those on Facebook — to bear any physical resemblance to either Greg or Jennifer. They were scattered all over the United States. One elderly Hugh Stiver resided in Uruguay.

My Hugh was elusive or reclusive — or perhaps had changed his name? I searched for Hugh Cutler, Cutler being the Stiver siblings' surname prior to the arrival in the household of Anson Stiver. Seven of these turned up; one was the right age, thirty-two. This Hugh Cutler was a mechanic at a garage in Arlington, Massachusetts. He had no Facebook page, and I found him through court records; Cutler was on probation following his conviction a year earlier for assault.

I phoned Jennifer Stiver. "Hey, thanks for your help today. I just have a quick question. Was your brother Hugh a mechanic?"

"Yes, but I can't talk to you anymore. I'm just too…ambivalent about what you're doing. I'm hanging up. Sorry."

And she was gone. So I couldn't ask her if she knew that Hugh apparently had a violent streak.

I finished the soup and salad.

I tried Virgil Jackman, reached his voice mail, and left no message.

Janie Insinger did answer her phone. She said she and Kev were "like, going out," and she could speak to me briefly.

"Just one question, Janie. When you were interviewed by the police after Greg's death, you told them he had been despondent. That was in the police report. Did you also mention his relationship with Kenyon Louderbush?"

"You bet we did. Why not? I was so ripshit, I didn't give a crap if he was some senator or if he was just some pissant geek."

"And the police noted this and asked you more about it? The physical abuse, for example…did that come up?"

"Sure, but this old bald guy detective — I forget his name — he just said that wasn't anything the cops could, like, get mixed up in. It was private. He said it used to be different, but nowadays the police didn't care about gay people and their private business. The new chief would just say it was none of the police's business."

"Uh-huh. Was this a Detective Nichols, do you remember?"

"Coulda been. He had hair coming out of his ears."

This would make him easy to find. Bald and hairy. "What about Greg's brother, Hugh? Did Greg ever talk about him to you? Hugh was a couple of years older."

"Greg had a brother? I didn't know that. Are you sure?"

"Yes. I heard about him from Jennifer. Hugh left Schenectady when he was eighteen."

"Greg never talked about him. They probably weren't close."

"Is Anthony still with you, the security guy from the campaign?"

"He's downstairs. Kev doesn't like him around, so we might give him the night off. Virgil probably would've tried to get him in the sack with us, but Kev is too straight for that, thank God."

"Well, be careful."

"You too."

I reread the police report. Why wasn't Insinger's mention of Louderbush in there? The cop would have known that

Louderbush was a big cheese in the Legislature, so apparently discretion had overridden conscientiousness.

My Blackberry alerted me that something had come in from Bud Giannopolous, and I checked the laptop. This was timely. The sizeable file was the Shenango Life Insurance Company report on the death of its policyholder, Gregory Stiver. The nine-page report by investigator Lorraine Fallon included the SUNY security and Albany Police findings and the APD verdict of suicide. In a "note to the files," Fallon wrote that a handwritten "addendum" to the police report labeled CONFIDENTIAL mentioned "a physically abusive male/male relationship" and "the possibility of foul play," rather than suicide. Fallon noted additionally, "Conversation with Nichols/APD. Suggest destroy copy. Unsubstantiated. Libelous? Leg. kahuna."

The copy of this handwritten addendum was missing from the insurance company's copy of the police report, as it was from my copy. The SUNY security report did include the scribbled note, "Call from Leg. Blessing responding." In her report, Fallon made no mention of this cryptic notation.

Fallon's "reluctant" recommendation to Shenango Life was to withhold paying the insurance policy's beneficiary, Jennifer Stiver, because the official verdict was suicide, and standard policy precluded a payout under such circumstances.

I went over this material twice again, and each time my attention snagged on the disappearing confidential memo about an abusive "Leg. kahuna," and on the "call from Leg." to which "Blessing" was to have responded.

I e-mailed Bud Giannopolous and asked him to please find out if SUNY had somebody on its staff named Blessing.

Then I called my pal at APD.

"I need to talk to a detective on the force named Ivor Nichols. Can you set something up?"

"Can't. Sorry. Ivor retired a couple of years ago. Even worse, both for him and for you, he passed away just last week."

"Crap."

"What's this about? Maybe I can help."

"What kind of cop was Nichols? Would he have altered a report to protect somebody important in the Legislature?"

"I guess you could say that Ivor was traditional in the regard. Yeah, I'd have to say so."

"What did he die of? Nothing violent, I hope."

"Lung cancer. It's not violent, technically speaking, although I've heard it feels that way."

CHAPTER TWELVE

I slept poorly. My back, legs and shoulders still ached, and the ear felt as if fire ants were gnawing at it. I had changed the bandage, per Albany Med's instructions, before I went to bed, and chowed down more Tylenol, all of this to not much effect.

When my wake-up call went off next to my flaming ear at five thirty Friday morning, I was already half conscious, half thinking and half dreaming about kahunas and Blessing and — go figure — an elegant blonde woman jumping into San Francisco bay. I showered without getting the bandage soaked, just splashed a little.

After throwing on some jeans and a polo shirt, I made my way down to the hotel parking garage, bringing along only my Blackberry and the Smith & Wesson in the shoulder bag. While the rental car appeared untampered-with, I gave the engine and wheel wells a quick once over.

Traffic was light at this early hour. I whizzed across the I-90 bridge and kept going east on the interstate, exiting briefly for a Dunkin' Donuts stop just past East Greenbush. I joined the orderly drive-thru queue — not wanting to go inside and frighten the bleary-eyed early morning customers with my repulsive hickey — and then got back on the highway and consumed the juice, coffee and bagel in the car. If anyone was tailing me, I was unaware of it, and I was staying watchful.

I didn't have my GPS with me, which left me feeling naked and helpless on the one hand, but also gratifyingly self-sufficient. I would stalk my prey using mainly my nose and also my vague recollection that Arlington, Massachusetts was located just west of Boston. I confirmed this on a map I picked up at a Massachusetts Turnpike service area and arrived in Arlington just in time to get stuck in the morning commuter traffic inching its way into the city.

As I crept along on state route 2, I found an NPR station on the radio and caught the tail end of a news report on upcoming primary elections across the US. The roundup mentioned in passing the New York State primary. The reporter said political handicappers were putting their money on the Tea Party-backed conservative Democrat Kenyon Louderbush. The Shy McCloskey campaign was described as "floundering." I said out loud, "You betcha."

I pulled into an Arlington Mobil station to ask directions to J&J's Auto Service, where Hugh Cutler worked, and was told that the Shell station diagonally across the intersection was J&J's. I made my way over there and filled the tank on the Hyundai. The station had no convenience store attached to it, just a two-bay garage, both doors up. I pulled over, out of the way of the comings and goings, and parked.

At the counter, a young guy with a rhinestone stud in his left ear and what looked like an incipient premature beer gut was giving an old lady the bad news about her alternator: kaput, big bucks to replace it. She looked downcast and said she would have to call "Mick." While she used the phone, I asked the counterman, whose name was Jim, according to some stitching on his work shirt pocket, if Hugh Cutler was there.

"Yeah. Why? Hugh's workin'."

"Need to talk. Department of Probation. This won't take long."

Jim took this in and didn't seem stunned. "What, like five minutes?"

"Or ten. No more."

He gave me a you-guys-drive-me-crazy-but-what-the-fuck-can-I-do look. "I'll get him."

I walked outside and stood on the far side of the rental car. Jim soon reappeared, followed by a frowning blue-eyed man with sandy hair over his collar, an unruly beard, and *Hugh* on his greasy work shirt.

"This won't take more than a few minutes," I said. "There's no problem. I just have a couple of questions."

Cutler looked apprehensive. Was I some new asshole he was going to have to deal with? "Okay. What questions?"

Jim turned and went back inside.

"This is actually unofficial." I showed him my ID. "I work out of Albany, New York and I'm looking into the circumstances of your brother Greg Stiver's death. I'm working for people who are very sympathetic to Greg and to your whole family situation. I've heard from your sister, Jennifer, how bad it was for both of you. I don't know how much you know about Greg's suicide."

He stared at me. "You're not from Probation?"

"Sorry about that. I thought your boss might be more inclined to let me talk to you for ten minutes."

"Yeah, and what if he didn't know about my status? Fuck."

"Well, he would. Those are the rules, I do believe. Anyway, I'll be out of here in no time."

"You sure as fuck will."

"I just wanted to find out what you knew about the suicide, and if you had been in touch with Greg around that time, and what he might have told you about what was going on in his head. And why you think he killed himself."

Hugh kept staring. "This is incredible. How did you even find me?"

"Court records. The assault conviction. I guessed that you might have changed your name from Stiver. Anson Stiver was a piss-poor excuse of a stepfather, I've heard from several people."

"I just can't believe this. I've had no contact with that family for fourteen years!"

"How did you know about Greg's death?"

"A buddy in Schenectady I stay in touch with e-mailed me. He saw it in the paper."

"I'm surprised that after you left Schenectady you didn't keep up contact with Greg. You were both victims of your stepfather's abuse. Or did you two also have some kind of falling out?"

His shoulders slumped a little. "Greg and I never talked to each other about anything. He went his way, and I went mine. He had school and all that stuff. I liked engines. There was nothing to fall out from. On my eighteenth birthday, I got out. And I never looked back."

"Your sister Jennifer is a teacher. She seems okay in her life."

"I know. My bud back home told me. Jenny never gave a fuck about me. She was like Mom. And I don't give a fuck about either one of them."

"You knew Greg was gay?"

"Yeah. He used to yell it around the house when he was in high school. It was a way to get back at Anson. But I couldn't care less whose pants he got into. That's the way Greg was, and so what?"

"Were you surprised when you heard he killed himself?"

Hugh leaned against the car and looked at the ground. "Yeah."

"He'd never seemed suicidal to you?"

"No. Greg was strong. I was really surprised when I heard that."

"In what ways was he strong?"

He thought about this. "I dunno. Just...he had a lot of ideas about the way things worked. He was like that kid on *Family Ties*. He was conservative and had all these Republican opinions. I really got tired of hearing it. That didn't seem very gay, but what do I know? Greg wanted to change the world, and he thought he could do it. That somebody who knows all that boring crap would just go ahead and kill themselves just didn't make sense to me."

"What were his gay relationships like? Were you aware of who he dated?"

"Not really. In high school he hung out with some other nerdy gays. A kid named Bootsy was kind of girly. I think they fooled around with each other, but Greg didn't have any big crushes or great loves that I ever saw. The only crush Greg had that I knew about was Ronald Reagan. Greg had a picture of Reagan on the wall in his room."

"What were your stepfather's politics? Or did he have any?"

"Dipped if I know. Anson hated all politicians. And everybody else, too."

"Was he violent with other people that you knew of? Or just you and Greg?"

A bitter look. "Why would Anson pound anybody else besides me and Greg? If it was a kid, he'd go to jail. If it was a grown-up, the dude might smack him back. No, he had it made, Anson did. I don't know who he must be knocking around now. I hate to think."

"Can I ask you about your assault conviction? What were the circumstances?"

He almost laughed. "You could figure it out."

"Maybe. What happened?"

"An asshole in a bar in Somerville. I was drunk. So was he. Big sack of shit, he starts ragging this kid, some Harvard dweeb, and he grabs the kid's glasses off and smashes them with his foot. The stupid kid is drunk too, and he pushes this guy, and the asshole slams the kid in the face and breaks his nose. That's when I lost it. I jumped the guy and pounded his head on the bar, and he ends up with a concussion. The cops come in and charge both of us with assault, and then we both get probation. Now I'm a criminal. Unlike Anson Stiver. Not fair, my man, not fair."

"Had you ever been violent before?"

He looked at me stonily. "Not really. Unless you count the day I left Schenectady."

"Anson?"

"I knocked out three of his front teeth. He never called the cops. The fucker knew better."

CHAPTER THIRTEEN

My room at the Crowne Plaza had been ransacked. Since I had hardly any belongings with me in the room — a small bag, a change of clothes, toiletries — this tossing stuff around was plainly for show. They wanted me to understand that they always knew where I was and how pathetically vulnerable I was.

My laptop was on the desk where I'd left it. So was the police report on the Stiver suicide that had been faxed to me. They — they being the Serbians? — hadn't taken the police report with them. Why? Because they already had a copy?

I powered up the laptop. It seemed fine. My password — *whyworry* — seemed to be the only thing the Serbians didn't know about me. My files were intact and the Internet connection blazed to life when I commanded it to do so. Still, I figured I'd have the McCloskey campaign's security techies check the computer out. Along with my car and…what? Our coffeemaker? Timmy's electric toothbrush?

How did they know where I was staying? I thought that I had not been followed from Crow Street to the hotel, but perhaps these people were such professionals and there were so many of them that I was simply helpless against their vast competence.

Down at the front desk, I asked the clerk if anybody had been looking for me over the past seven hours. The well-manicured young man perused his counter area, looked back up at my bandaged ear and said no. There was no point in telling him that my room had been broken into. I was the only person with a coded key card that could open the door to room 612. Just the maid and I, and anybody else who could hack into the hotel's computer system and retrieve my room number and card code.

"Will you be staying with us another night, sir?" the clerk asked.

"Yes, I will," I lied, and thought about where I might actually spend the night where the Serbians would not be able to find me.

Back in the room, I ordered a Cobb salad from room service and called Timmy. He wasn't answering, so I left a message saying I was back in Albany from Massachusetts and would be in touch.

My Blackberry got excited, and it was a message from Bud Giannopolous. He said there was a Blessing at SUNY, a Millicent Blessing in the public information office. I called there and was told that Ms. Blessing would be leaving the office in a short while and perhaps I could have an appointment with her next week. I explained that I was with BBC America and we were on a tight schedule, and it would be so great if my crew and I could drop by that afternoon. I was put on hold briefly, then informed that an afternoon interview would be feasible.

I got Tom Dunphy on the phone.

"I'm waving at you. Can you see me?"

"No. The windows over there are tinted. You're still at the Crowne Plaza?"

"One more night. Two at the most." I told him about the break-in at my hotel room. "These people are amazing, Tom. They see me when I'm sleeping. They know when I'm awake. They know when I've been bad or good. So, what's going on, for fuck's sake?"

I could hear another phone going off nearby, but Dunphy stayed with me. "This does sound very professional on Louderbush's part. Too professional. It's almost like it's the feds or something. I'm trying to puzzle this out. It is too, too peculiar."

"The feds don't try to rip people's ears off or slash their tires. If they want to intimidate somebody, they are generally subtler in the way they go about it. Anyway, why would federal agents care if Kenyon Louderbush is a total asshole, or why would they even know about any of this? No, this is somebody else with an interest in the primary campaign, probably Louderbush's people themselves. Who's your counterpart over at their campaign?"

"Leonard Sample. Len's young and crass and an anti-Obama true believer. I'd be surprised, though, if Len resorted to violence. He's a religious guy and pious as shit. His violent tendencies are all in his policy ideas."

"Oh? Maybe I'll keep an open mind about that."

"Of course, you should."

I told Dunphy I was going out to pick up my car with its four new tires — these would show up on my expense statement — and I'd like Clean-Tech to check out the vehicle for tracking or listening devices and also my laptop for any weirdness.

"Come by the office later this afternoon, and I'll get some of their geniuses over here. Five o'clock?"

"Make it the Crowne Plaza garage. I'm being watched, and I want it known that I am not alone in this and we have a veritable righteous army at our disposal. They can scare me off, but twenty more just like me will pick up the baton."

Dunphy took this seriously. "The campaign can't afford twenty more like you, Don, but I take your point."

I ate half my Cobb salad, then had to get up and get going. I drove out to Schenectady on Route 5, assuming I was being followed but not caring overly much. I returned the rental car and picked up my Toyota with its shiny new tires. The tab came to $712 for the tires, towing, and so on, an unanticipated expenditure for donors to the Shy McCloskey gubernatorial campaign. It was up to me — and maybe only me? — to see that they got their money's worth.

Heading back to Albany on the interstate, I took the Washington Avenue SUNY exit and made my way to the administration building that housed the public information office. No one seemed to be following me. I checked the skies overhead for miniature drone aircraft with cameras but didn't spot any.

I identified myself to the department receptionist and said, "I'd like to talk to Ms. Blessing, if I may. It has to do with the death of a student five years ago."

She nodded sympathetically. "I'll check with Millie. People are coming from BBC America to interview her, but they haven't shown up yet."

"I'll try to be quick."

I was soon ushered into an office like Paul Podolski's — spare design, functional gizmos, bookish clutter — except three times the size of his and with a couch. A window looked out on the spot half the length of a rugby field away where Greg Stiver had fallen to his death.

Millicent Blessing, stylish and fiftyish, with a ready smile and a firm round bottom, offered her hand and said, "I'll be happy to talk to you, Mr. Strachey, but it's really the lawyers who the McTavishes should be in touch with. At this point, we're all at the mercy of Chilton, Quarrels and whatever they might work out with the McTavishes' law firm. Or is that who you're representing?"

"Who are the McTavishes? What's their involvement? I'm confused."

"Oh. Gail said death of a student. Is this about something else?"

I took a seat, as did Blessing, now looking a bit tentative about my presence.

"I'm making some inquiries for a client about graduate student Gregory Stiver's suicide five years ago. I understand you were here at the time."

The smile melted away and Blessing may actually have blanched. "Oh yes, I remember that. It was horrible. I was thinking of another death on campus. One more recent — a binge drinking tragedy. But, yes, Gregory Stiver. That one was heartbreaking, just heartbreaking."

"Greg was about to receive his master's degree. All that achievement, and then he jumped to his death. From that building just over there, I understand. The Quad Four tower."

She blinked back tears. "That's right. The awful thing is…. It's hard to talk about this, but the terrible thing is, I was here in the office at the time sitting right at my desk where I am now.

And if I had looked out the window a few seconds later than I did, I might actually have seen Gregory fall. I think — I'm saying I *think* — I noticed him on the roof before he jumped off of it. But I didn't make anything of it. I suppose I just assumed it was university maintenance people up there. Then a couple of minutes later there were security staff and the police and the ambulance, and that's when I went down there. I saw that boy's broken body. It was a sight I'll never forget. It was devastating, just devastating."

"You said you might have seen what might have been maintenance people on the roof. People, plural. Not just Greg?"

"Maybe. I don't really know. There was so much confusion at the time, I wasn't really sure what I saw or when I saw it. I thought about it afterward, trying to remember. But I do have this image in my head that I can't get rid of, of two people on the Quad Four roof before the thing happened. That's all it is, just a kind of blurry image, like a picture that's out of focus."

"In your image, what were the two people doing?"

She sighed. "God, I wish I knew. Nothing. Just standing or — I don't know. Working on the roof? Of course, maybe I just imagined I saw anything at all. I told the police detective about what I thought I remembered, and he said nobody else had reported seeing anything similar. He said it seemed as though it was just Gregory on the roof, because his backpack was up there and his cell phone. And of course if anybody else was there at the time, presumably they would have tried to stop Gregory from jumping, and then they would have reported whatever they knew about the whole hideous situation."

"Do you remember the police detective's name?"

"I don't, really. He was a middle-aged man with male-pattern baldness. Rather emotionless. I remember thinking he wasn't just stoic but rather cold."

"Could it have been Detective Ivor Nichols?"

"Oh. I think it was. Ivor is an unusual name for an Albany police officer."

"He was the investigating officer. I can't ask him about his own recollections because Detective Nichols died a couple of weeks ago."

"I'm sorry to hear that. Was his passing work-related?"

"Lung cancer."

"So not work-related, exactly. Though you have to wonder how much cancer is triggered by stress."

"Or the nicotine and tar a lot of people still employ to cope with stress."

"I smoked in college. Nicotine is such a powerful drug. I can't say I think about it much anymore. But if there's an afterlife and smoking is allowed, I'd be tempted to take it up again. What harm would there be in it at that point?"

"Sounds awfully good to me. How much," I asked, "did you know about Greg Stiver's personal life? Apparently it had been stressful in the months before his death."

"I knew very little. The police looked into that. Apparently friends of Gregory talked about job-hunting difficulties. I know he was gay, but there was no evidence that he was bullied or anything like that. Nothing that I heard about, or that the police mentioned. And there was a suicide note, the police said."

"Yes. Although I don't know where that note is today. Three people saw it, and where it went after that is unclear."

"Why, may I ask, are you looking into Greg's death five years after it happened? Does this have something to do with insurance? There were no legal complications at the time involving the university. The stairwell door had been left unlocked, but no one at the time made anything of that at all. If someone is determined to jump from a high place, they can easily find somewhere to do it."

"There are some lingering questions about a relationship Greg was in and whether or not its abusive nature contributed to his taking his own life."

"Oh no. How horrible."

"It's murky, but apparently there was something violent going on with another gay man that contributed to Greg's despondency."

"So are legal proceedings underway? I mean, what's the statute of limitations on something like that? And who are you conducting this investigation for?"

"My clients are people sympathetic to Greg and his fate."

"His family?"

"No, they're a bit of a conundrum in all this."

"I don't know that they ever contacted the university after Gregory's death. I'm trying to recall, but I think I heard that his belongings stayed with the campus police and no one ever picked them up."

"Might campus security still have them? His backpack? His phone?"

"You'd have to ask. I can tell you who to talk to over there."

"There's one puzzling note on the campus cops' report, which I've seen. The note says *Call from Leg.* That's L-E-G-period. Then it says *Blessing responding.* What was that about? Did L-E-G mean Legislature?"

She didn't flinch or turn white again. "Hmm. It probably meant Legislature. Our office is involved with university relations with the Assembly, the Senate and the governor's office. It's entirely possible someone from the Legislature contacted me about the circumstances of Gregory's death. Maybe an assemblyman or senator who knew the family. I have no memory of it, but that doesn't mean it didn't happen. You know, I could check. My notes on the incident are in our system."

"Would you? That'd be great."

"Then, Mr. Strachey, I'm afraid I can't spare you any additional time. BBC America is sending a crew out to interview me. I assume it's for something they're doing on budget cuts or tuition increases. Budgetarily, we're under the gun like never before. The Brits are, too, so I suppose they want to know how were handling the financial crunch."

"Probably."

She fooled around with her computer for a minute or two, scrolling up and down, this way and that.

"Here it is," she said finally. "Assemblyman Louderbush's office called asking for a copy of the campus police report. Security knows that we liaise with the Assembly, so they passed on the request to us. I'm sure I sent the report, as per the request. It is odd, though. Isn't Mr. Louderbush's district out in the western part of the state? Gregory was from Schenectady."

"He was."

"And now Kenyon Louderbush is running for governor. Mister Tea Party. Your investigation has nothing to do with that, does it?"

"That remains to be seen."

Now she was starting to look apprehensive. "What happened to your ear?"

I gave her a quick rundown on the ex-girlfriend. She seemed skeptical, but before I left she did give me the name of the campus police official who might know where Greg Stiver's phone and backpack could be found.

CHAPTER FOURTEEN

At first, the campus cop didn't want to look for the stuff. It was in a room he didn't have a key for. And the guy with the key was on his break. I asked where the break was taking place, and I tracked the officer down in a cafeteria. He couldn't give me the key, of course — even though I was Gregory Stiver's Uncle Donald — but he said he'd be returning to the office in ten minutes. I sat down and watched him read the *New York Post*.

"Yanks are for shit this year."

"Looks that way."

In the office, I was required to sign something certifying I was a Stiver family member. I did so and walked off with Greg Stiver's backpack. I checked to see if the cell phone was in it. It was, along with books and other items.

I had a number of chargers in the car and found one that fit Stiver's five-year-old Verizon phone. It was just a telephone, no aromatherapy apps or IMAX. I charged the phone while I drove downtown.

Back in the hotel room, I checked the phone first. There were eighteen stored numbers and I made a note of each. The only ones that rang a bell were Jenny, Prof P, and KL. I guessed KL was not Kuala Lumpur but Kenyon Louderbush. Moreover, the last number called from this phone five years earlier was the one listed for KL.

Otherwise the backpack yielded nothing useful. It contained a copy of Stiver's thesis, two books on economic theory, a copy of the *National Review* and a half-full bottle of drinking water. There was no notebook or other more personal item. The Albany cops had undoubtedly been through the bag, so it was possible some of its contents had been removed.

I phoned Timmy, who answered this time. I asked him if everyone in his office was frantic, what with the state budget many weeks overdue and the state coming close to running on empty.

"Very funny."

"Right. It is Friday afternoon."

"Myron's on his way into the city, and the rest of us are sitting around figuring out ways to add some generous new perks to our pension plans."

This was a joke, for Timmy's boss, Assemblyman Lipschutz, had led countless fights to reform both the nonsensically overstuffed state budget and the way the Legislature was a mere plaything for the corporate and union lobbyists who underwrote election campaigns. None of these reform efforts had come close to succeeding, and Shy McCloskey had pledged his support for another reform go-round. He may even have been sincere.

I brought Timmy up to date on my visit with Hugh Cutler, who had been surprised that his estranged brother had killed himself, and on my meeting with Millicent Blessing, who believed she had seen two people on the roof of Quad Four just before Greg Stiver plunged to his death.

"So is it looking as if Stiver's death wasn't actually suicide? That's unnerving."

"I don't know. As it adds up, the evidence keeps coming back to that possibility. It's hard to imagine, though, that anybody — Louderbush or anybody else — would have pushed Stiver off a building in broad daylight. It's true that it all happened while classes were in session, and you know how deserted a college campus can become while everybody is indoors taking notes and trying hard not to look at their watches more than once every five minutes. But there are always a few people out and about, so any kind of rooftop confrontation would be tremendously risky for anybody intent on foul play."

"Of course, foul play isn't often intended. Sometimes it just happens."

"There's that, yes. Maybe especially among people with a history of violent behavior between them."

"Also, how tall is the building?"

"Eight stories."

"So anything happening on the roof wouldn't be visible from down below unless it was happening at the very edge. Witnesses would have to be some distance from the building to have a view of any activity on the roof. And that distance would make it hard to make out what was going on."

"Hence Millicent Blessing's uncertainty over what she saw."

"But," Timmy said, "if it wasn't suicide, how at this late date — or anytime — would anybody know what the truth was without having been there at the time? Only the other person on the roof — if there was another person — would know what really happened. So, are you feeling kind of at a dead end in this?"

"My assignment is to find out if Kenyon Louderbush really did have an abusive relationship with Greg Stiver, and if so, might it have contributed to his death? Figuring that out still seems doable, even though the only two witnesses so far, Janie Insinger and Virgil Jackman, are far from perfect as credible moral finger pointers, and Janie is unlikely to go public at all. I'm convinced, though, that Louderbush did do something very, very bad — so bad that the Serbians keep trying to scare me off the case. So I have to keep slogging. This guy has to be stopped."

"Louderbush plus his Balkan gangsters."

"Well, whoever the bastards were who beat me up and wrecked my tires and ransacked my room."

Now he was paying even closer attention. "What do you mean, ransacked your room?"

"Oh, didn't I mention that? While I was in Massachusetts this morning. They got into my room at the hotel."

"God, how did they do that? Those rooms are supposed to be secure."

"They're supposed to be."

Timmy fussed for a few minutes over my physical vulnerability, and then asked, "Do you have your gun with you?"

"I do."

"I don't know why that makes me feel worse, not better. Well, I do know why. As I have pointed out previously, it's the statistics."

"It's true that statistically handguns are far more of a risk to their owners than to the average violent criminal. But you know me. Remember, in college I got a C in statistics."

"Oh, well, then. So was anything taken from your room?"

"No, the break-in was just more mau-mau-style waving of bones and feathers in my face. They want me off the case, and this was part of their instant-message booga-booga routine."

"They must be wondering what it would take to actually get you to throw in the towel. Or, maybe they aren't wondering that at all. Maybe their aim in threatening and harassing you is entirely different."

"Like what?"

"I don't know."

"These guys do seem to be holding back. But they let me know constantly that they're on top of my every move. Clean-Tech is going to check the car for a tracking device, and they'll go over my laptop, too."

"How's your ear? And your big hickey?"

"The ear hurts. The hickey is sexy as all get out."

"Will you stay at the hotel tonight? If the Louderbush gang knows your every move, why not just come home? We can keep a cauldron of boiling XVOO at a second floor window in case the Croatians start marching up Crow Street."

"Serbians. No, let's keep you and the house out of this. I'll let you know where I end up."

"Be careful."

"Yep."

It was nearly five, and I grabbed my laptop and took the elevator down to the hotel parking garage. A white Clean-Tech van was waiting near the entrance, and out stepped Tom Dunphy and two stringy gimlet-eyed men in sports jackets. A fourth man drove the van as I led them all down one level to where my Toyota was parked. I handed the computer over to one of the solemn guys, who climbed into the back of the van with it. The other man had a black box with a wire and a wand, and he began waving it around my car. The van's driver got out, and he opened all the doors on the Toyota and popped both the hood and the trunk.

While these guys worked, I stepped into the shadows of the garage with Dunphy. I watched other cars come and go while we talked. Nobody looked our way or stopped. No Serbians appeared, or Croatians or Roma.

Dunphy told me the McCloskey campaign was creeping ahead but was having trouble raising money because Louderbush was draining off a good bit of cash in the Buffalo area. And even downstate around heavily Democratic New York City, donations were down. Too many Dems assumed Louderbush would win the primary and Ostwind the general, and a dank fatalism had set in. Big givers were already looking ahead to other electoral races two years down the road. It was becoming more and more critical, Dunphy said, that Louderbush be forced to drop out of the gubernatorial contest soon. Otherwise, just around the bend lay colossal ruin.

I gave Dunphy an update on my findings, including the report from Millicent Blessing that Louderbush's office had made inquiries about the Stiver suicide soon after it happened, even though Stiver was not Louderbush's constituent and his district was over 200 miles from Stiver's Albany residence.

Dunphy said, "That's evidence of something, it sounds like."

"It seems to be. Why were his staff people asking? I'd love to find out. You don't happen to have a mole working in Louderbush's office, do you?"

"No, we don't. A dirty trick like that would be wrong."

Why did he talk like this? "Tom, you aren't wearing a wire,

are you?"

"Of course not. Why would you ask that?"

"It's my Walmart training."

"You worked for Walmart?"

The guys checking my car out came over and said they couldn't find any tracking or listening device. They said a more thorough search in their shop could be arranged but was unlikely to yield a different result. They were certain no electronic transmissions were being broadcast from anywhere in my car.

This was a relief in the sense that I could now drive my own car and not have to worry about leading Louderbush operatives to my every encounter. But it was disappointing in that I still had no idea how these people always seemed to know exactly where I was at any given moment.

The computer man returned my laptop and said it didn't seem infected in any way, and my files had not been accessed except via my own password.

"There is some gay porn in there," the guy said. "I have to mention that in case you didn't know it was there. College wrestlers in sexual activity with teammates?"

"I'm aware of that material."

"That's up to you. It's not uncommon. And this is your own PC, not a government apparatus, so it's your business."

"True enough."

Dunphy said, "Gay college wrestlers. Holy jeez. I'm sure that wasn't the case at Williams."

The Clean-Tech crew departed, and Dunphy said he would make his own way back down the hill to his office. I walked with him out to State Street, and he asked me what was next according to my plan of attack.

I said I wasn't sure, but I knew I needed to chase down any additional witnesses I could find to the Stiver-Louderbush abusive relationship. I said I also wanted to talk to Stiver's parents, if possible, and anybody else who might offer insights into Stiver's intentions and his state of mind in the weeks and days before his death. I planned, too, on checking out the college where Stiver's thesis advisor said he'd been offered a job after he supposedly told others that he had been rejected twice for teaching positions.

"That all sounds," Dunphy said, "as if it might take a while. I'm getting nervous as hell that by the time you nail this guy to the cross — and eventually I'm sure you will nail him — by that time Merle Ostwind will be up there at the top of State Street hill with her pretty little white-lady right hand raised up in the chill January air being sworn in as New York State's next governor. Can you speed this up just a wee bit, Don? God, tempus is fucking fugiting. Can you understand the position we're in here? Well, of course you can. And I know you can do this job for us. I've heard that about you. That and all kinds of other good things.   Mister-Get-the-Job-Done-One-Way-or-Another.   Just do it faster, please, if you don't mind my saying so. I'm putting pressure on you, and pressure is good. Grace under pressure. That's all I'm insisting on. Grace and, more importantly, speed. Can I make it any plainer?"

I said, "Dunphy, I think you need to walk across the street to Jack's for happy hour and take a load off. You're unraveling and that's not helping. In the meantime, either keep me on the payroll to finish this job as fast as I can humanly do it, or fire my ass and bring Pinkerton in, or Rudy Giuliani, or Captain Marvel. Think it over. I'll be in touch."

I left him on the sidewalk looking alone and dejected, and I felt pretty rotten myself. In fact, I had no idea what exactly to do next. I rode back up to my room, popped more Tylenol — the earache had seemed to spread deep into my brain — and stuffed my meager belongings into my bag and prepared to head off to — where?

My cell phone rang.

"This is Strachey."

A long pause. I noted the number calling me, and I saw that it was the same number that was stored in Greg Stiver's phone as belonging to KL.

I said, "Take your time. I know who you are."

More static. Then, weakly, "How could you know who I am?"

"Your number was stored in Greg Stiver's cell. I saw it there."

More static. Where was he calling from? Finland?

He said, "I need to talk to you."

"Sure. That could be helpful."

"No. I just need to explain. You don't understand *any* of this."

"Okay."

"Can we meet? Privately?"

"Yes, we can. My house on Crow Street?"

His voice was the one I'd heard countless times on television going on about horrible big government and out-of-control taxes, but now the voice was wobbly and a bit hard to make out. He said, "No, outside of Albany somewhere. Where we can talk and I won't run into anybody."

"There's a Motel 6 on Route 7 just east of Troy. I'll get a room."

Another pause. "I suppose that would work."

"Seven o'clock?"

"No, it's better after dark. Ten is better. Ten o'clock."

"My car will be parked in front of my room. I'll tape a note to the door that says *Don*." I described my car and gave Louderbush the license number.

"I've got that. Thank you. Thank you so much."

"Will you be coming alone, Assemblyman?"

"Absolutely. That's the whole point."

"Right. See you at ten."

He rang off and I wondered how I was going to sit still for the next three and a half hours.

CHAPTER FIFTEEN

Louderbush didn't show. I sat waiting, my Smith & Wesson under a pillow — precautions wouldn't do any harm — and kept on waiting for over half an hour. At ten forty I dialed Louderbush's number and got his voicemail.

I said, "I understand this is no picnic for you. But your impulse in calling me was a decent one. You said you wanted to explain. I'm ready to listen. So please call again, and we'll do what we need to do to get this sorted out. I hope to speak with you soon."

What was Louderbush up to? He seemed to be presenting himself as the aggrieved party here, the fellow who was being misunderstood. But how could he possibly come up with a story that cast himself in any kind of positive light? I didn't get it, but I was immensely curious.

I took the *Don* sign down from my door and locked myself in. Through the motel's thin walls, I could hear a TV going in the next room, one of those hair-raising real housewives shows that leaves you convinced civilization is basically over and a kind of human devolution is well underway.

I phoned Janie Insinger and asked if she was safe and doing all right. She said she was, but she sounded tipsy and she asked if she could speak to me some other time because at that moment she and Kevin and Anthony were "like, having a party."

When I called Virgil Jackman, he said he was just getting off work, and he hadn't been bothered by any Serbians either. He said he was going out with Kimberly and he would talk to me Monday if that was okay. I said sure.

It was Friday night, so maybe even the Serbians were out doing the club scene.

I reached Timmy at home, and all was well there. I told him where I was and what had happened with Kenyon Louderbush.

"Wow."

"You bet."

"Maybe he knows you're on his trail, and he's going to drop out of the race."

"I doubt it. He wouldn't do it through me. He'd just announce he had a brain tumor, or he wanted to spend more time with his family, or a voice had spoken to him in the night and told him to move to Salt Lake City."

"You're right. These guys never just spit it out."

"No, Louderbush seems to think of me as somebody who can somehow defuse the accusation. I want to hear his story, and I'm irked that he didn't show up at the motel. But this thing was plainly eating at him, and I'm guessing he'll call again."

"So, are you spending the night up there?"

"Yeah, and I think I've finally shaken the Serbians loose. I checked out of the Crowne Plaza. Maybe I'll be back home tomorrow night. It's possible Louderbush has called off the dogs while he tries to negotiate something. Not that there's anything to negotiate, really, if he admits to having had a physically abusive affair with Greg Stiver."

"Maybe Louderbush was the second person somebody saw on the roof with Stiver, and he shoved the kid off in a rage, and now he wants to confess."

"That's disgusting and tidy and not altogether implausible, but the confession part seems unlikely. What he said to me was that I didn't understand, and he wanted to explain what happened. That doesn't sound like a confession in the offing. It sounds like a defense."

"Let's hope he calls back soon."

"Not tonight necessarily. I'm beat. And I still hurt all over. I guess I should change the dressing on my ear again. Maybe even have it checked. It feels as if something is gnawing at the side of my head. Rats or ferrets."

"This is becoming too graphic for me. I may have to go watch the Oprah channel. Should I come up there? I could be in Troy in fifteen minutes. I hate it when you don't feel good. It's so unlike you. Maybe I could cheer you up in some familiar way."

"Thanks, lover, but Tylenol will have to do. What I really need is to go right to sleep."

"Tomorrow then."

"It's a plan."

Except, when I turned the lights out, I couldn't sleep. The whole ugly mess kept sloshing around in my aching head. I could hear the housewives sniping and puling in the next room. Didn't anybody who stayed in motels ever watch the Hallmark Channel? I turned on the TV in my room while the eleven o'clock news was on but didn't see or hear a thing. I was aware enough to know there was no local political news on, just car wrecks, fires, cats with cancer stories, weather — rain was on the way — and baseball. I shut off the TV when Jay Leno came on but still couldn't sleep.

At a quarter to twelve, I got up, fired up my laptop and went over my notes. They were blurry and indistinct. Had I developed an ear infection that had spread to my brain? I wasn't feverish but I still felt ill and impaired. I gave up on the notes, turned off the bedside light and opened the college wrestler download, *Humpy Mat Humpers*. That was good for about ten minutes, leaving me even more exhausted and still wide awake.

A cell phone whose ring tone was Queen's *We Are the Champions* went off in the room on the other side of me — the housewives on my right had called it a night — and a woman's voice cried out with delight, "Junior!" Then Junior got an earful. Mom had gotten her hair tinted and Midge had had her baby, and I got an earful, too.

I turned on Leno, switched to Letterman, then to TCM. *Casablanca* was on, and I recited the lines along with the actors. I had read recently that Bogart and Ingrid Bergman hadn't liked each other. She considered him boorish, he found her haughty — and this sad thought left me even more anxious and depressed.

When the movie ended, I started channel surfing and was

clicking by a couple of religious channels when a phrase snagged my attention and I stopped. A wizened preacher with tanning-booth skin and a gray pompadour was telling a blond lady with a painted smile about something he called the Eddie Fund. As I listened, it became clear that this was a ministry whose purpose was to turn gay people straight through counseling and prayer. When the phone number viewers could call in order to make a donation was shown, I made a note of it. Just twenty-five dollars would make Jesus smile, viewers were told. Old JC and his famous lopsided grin.

Soon the preacher changed the subject, and I turned off the set. As I drifted into a restless sleep, I wondered why, when out-and-proud Log Cabin Republican Greg Stiver had died, mourners were asked to donate to a religious crackpot cure-a-gay organization. This made no sense, unless of course the person in charge of funeral arrangements had been Anson Stiver, the evil stepfather. Him, I had to meet.

CHAPTER SIXTEEN

Rain pounded down in drops the size of boccie balls. I cupped a hand over my injured ear and made it out to the car with my laptop and overnight bag. I got in and slammed the door.

Then I saw the note on the windshield. I climbed back out, grabbed the piece of sopping paper, and got back inside. The ink had run, but the handwritten two-word message was still legible. *I'm sorry.*

So Louderbush had shown up sometime during the night and left this apology? Presumably the note was his. Only two people knew where I was staying: Louderbush and Timmy. It seemed as if Louderbush had called off the Serbians, and he was trying to somehow deal with the repulsive mess he'd made, but he kept losing his nerve. I tried to work up some sympathy for him, but it was hard to find any.

I made a quick Dunkin' Donuts stop in Troy and headed back down the river to Albany, eating and drinking in the car, and trying to find any political news on the radio. WAMC had on a few local headlines; none mentioned Kenyon Louderbush or the gubernatorial campaign.

I thought about driving out to Hall Creek Community College, where Paul Podolski said Stiver had had a teaching job lined up, but I decided to wait until Monday. It seemed unlikely I'd find anybody out there willing and able to talk to me on a Saturday morning in June.

Instead, I headed toward Schenectady. I had an address for Anson and Margery Stiver. I pulled into the breakdown lane and keyed the address into my GPS. Normally I would have done this while in motion — another distracted-driving asshole — but I still felt so crummy that I feared that any greater than usual distraction might end in calamity.

The Anson Stiver home in Schenectady was in one of the nicer neighborhoods in this sad-ass abandoned-by-GE old rust-belt town. Ridgemont Drive was probably where company managers and professional people had made their comfortable lives from the nineteen-teens up until the seventies, when the company moved south and way, way east. The Stivers' ample manse was fieldstone below, powder blue wood frame above, with white decorative shutters and a big white front door with a bronze knocker. The front lawn wasn't as well tended as others in the neighborhood, and the azaleas needed pruning.

A blue Chevy Suburban was parked in the driveway in front of the Stivers' unopened garage doors. I pulled in next to it and made a dash through the rain for the front door. There wasn't much of an overhang, and after making a couple of noisy bangs with the knocker I stood as close to the door as I could without risking ending up nose-to-nose with whoever might suddenly appear. Nothing happened for the next two minutes, and my back and shoulders were getting wet. This was quite the passive-aggressive residential portal. I knocked again and tried the doorbell, too. The mailbox next to the door appeared to be empty, but I didn't go poking around in it.

The door swung open, and a woman who looked unprepared for guests stood peering out at me. She looked more rained on than I did. Her pale gray eyes were soft, but the face around them was an Okefenokee of channels and rivulets, the uneasily-lived-in middle-aged face of a woman who was beyond vanity out of choice or otherwise. She had on a pink terrycloth bathrobe, with another pink towel wrapped around her head. A few strands of wet gray hair stuck out from under the wrap.

"I thought this might be the cable people, or I wouldn't have answered it. You're not with Time Warner?"

"I'm sorry, no. I'm here about your son. I take it you're Margery Stiver?"

"About Hugh?" She looked frightened. "What about Hugh? Is he all right?"

"Actually, Hugh is doing okay. I saw him yesterday. It's your late son, Gregory, I'd like to talk to you about if you have a few minutes. I apologize for barging in like this, Mrs. Stiver."

She relaxed a little. "Where did you see Hugh? Did he say for you to come here?"

"No, he didn't. I didn't tell him I would be talking to you. I was asking him some things about Greg. May I come in for just a few minutes? I know you're expecting Time Warner." I showed her my ID.

"Oh. A private investigator?"

"Licensed by the state of New York."

"You saw Hugh. Yes, okay, you can come in. My husband is in the other room. He's busy."

She led me through a foyer past a carpeted staircase and into what used to be called a den and maybe still was west of Crow Street. A flat-screen TV the size of a Caddie Escalade occupied one wall, and the bookshelves lining another held what appeared to be collectible plates with an early American motif on wooden stands and a couple of shelves of mystery novels that included the complete works of Margaret Truman.

"I'm so glad you saw Hugh. I have to say I'm envious," Mrs. Stiver added with a nervous laugh. "I haven't seen Hugh for going on fourteen years." She perched on the edge of a long low couch while I seated myself tentatively on a well-worn recliner I assumed was that of her husband, the child beater. The only printed matter on the coffee table was the Sunday *Times Union* TV listings. "I suppose Hugh told you that he's estranged from his family — from Anson and myself."

"Yes, he did. That must be very difficult, especially for you." She didn't pick up on this.

"How is he? What is he doing? Is he a mechanic? Hugh was the handy one with machines and engines."

"He's an auto mechanic."

"In Massachusetts?"

"Yes."

"A friend of mine, Cindy Visnicki, saw him there three or four years ago. I wrote to an address a friend of Cindy's got hold of, but Hugh never wrote back. He hates us." She didn't sob or tear up. She just looked at me, waiting, it seemed, to find out how much I knew.

I said, "Hugh's childhood was pretty bad, is my impression. Apparently he prefers to leave it far behind."

"I know. I understand. I don't blame him."

"No."

"I suppose I could blame myself."

"Oh?"

"But what's the point?"

"It's hard to know."

"You can do what you can do, but you can only do what you can do."

"Mm."

"Doctor Phil says self-reproach can eat you alive if you let it. Move on and get it right the next time. That's what I've tried to do."

There seemed to be no point asking her if she planned on having three more children and raising them in a home without a sadist in it. "Does your husband also have regrets about the way the boys were treated?"

She sniffed. "I really wouldn't know what Anson thinks about my children. Or about anything else."

"He's the uncommunicative type?"

"Uncommunicative? With the boys, Anson communicated with his fists. With Jennifer and me — Jennifer is my daughter — he didn't have much to say, no. What Anson was, was a good provider. I never had that as a child, and my husband Jim was also a disappointment in that way. He died at age thirty-one when he spent a good part of his paycheck one Friday night on beer and on losing at poker and then driving a company pickup truck into a bridge abutment. Snyder Construction didn't only refuse to pay for the last three days Jim worked. They thought I should also reimburse them for the truck. Can you believe it?"

"You were in a fix."

"Anson was just coming out of a divorce, and we were both feeling incredibly lost and needy, and he had his engineering job at GE. And of course he never told me why his first wife had left him and moved to California along with their two little boys. I only heard about that later on."

"I see."

"Hugh knew you were from Albany, I guess?"

"Yes, I told him I was."

"Did he ask you anything about me?"

"No, I'm sorry to say he didn't. He seems to have moved on, too."

"I see Jenny once in a while. She's strong like Gregory was. Hugh was the cutie, but Jenny would never take any guff from anybody. And Greg — that boy always knew exactly what he wanted. He seemed to end up with Anson's brains and determination even though Anson was not his biological father. I really thought Gregory would go far. When he died, I was so, so torn up. It wasn't just that he was gone, but I really didn't believe he was someone who would take his own life. It made not one shred of sense to me. It just wasn't who Greg was. I kept saying, no, they must have him mixed up with somebody else who would commit suicide. I mean, somebody who survived Anson Stiver would then just *give up*? It drove me crazy trying to figure it all out. And I never did. I never ever understood why Greg died the way he did."

"Some of his friends say he had been depressed in the weeks leading up to his death. This was possibly related to his not landing a teaching job. Though someone else has told me he did eventually find a position at a community college near Rochester. Did you know about any of this?"

Her voice wobbled. "No. By that time, Greg wasn't in touch with us a whole lot. Jenny was, but Anson and I weren't in touch with him at all, really. Jenny was on Greg's life insurance policy, as you know. So is Shenango finally going to pay Jenny what they owe her? She has all those student loans, and Anson says we can't help out because we only just get by. The one good thing about Greg not being here now is he doesn't have to see what Obama has done to the economy."

"I'm not involved with Shenango Life, Mrs. Stiver. But my client is very sympathetic to Greg and wants some kind of justice done regarding his death."

"Oh, I assumed you were an insurance investigator. You're not?"

"No. Anyway, once a death has officially been ruled a suicide, insurance companies are generally off the hook. Otherwise, people planning on killing themselves could just take out big life insurance policies before dying and all but bankrupt the industry."

She rolled her eyes. "The insurance companies won't get any sympathy from me. They're all just greedy. And now they're going to make out like bandits with Obamacare."

I said, "I know you knew that Greg was gay."

"Oh yes. How could we not know it? The whole world knew it. Greg saw to that. I was accepting, of course. I believe that some people are born that way. My first husband Jim had a brother we all wondered about. Anson was not accepting, though. He thought Greg became gay just to get even with him, but that's just foolishness. For an engineer, Anson has a few strange unscientific opinions."

"Was it your husband who requested that donations in Greg's memory be made to something called the Eddie Fund? That was listed in the newspaper obituaries."

She turned as pink as the towel on her head. "I did not know at the time what kind of organization that was. Anson knew I would not have approved. He said it was something about orphans. Then Jenny found out what it really was, and she had a fit."

"Were you aware of any of Greg's gay relationships? Who he

dated?"

"Just in high school. An effeminate boy named Bootsy was always coming over and spending time in Greg's room with him. But then Anson caught them doing something, and that was the end of that. In college, Greg was off on his own. I thought maybe he had a boyfriend who would show up at the funeral and I would get to meet him. But that didn't happen as far as I know. I was disappointed. I always hoped that unlike myself, Greg would find real love with another adult person."

Mrs. Stiver showed no emotion when she said this. It was just a fact of her life, one of a number she had accepted before mentally moving on.

I pondered telling her that Greg had in fact found a kind of intimacy with another man. And although this intimacy was mixed with love, it was also twisted and masochistic and almost certainly directly related to the abuse Stiver had suffered for years at the hands of his stepfather. I decided not to drop this on her for the time being. My dredging up all the ugliness she preferred not to think about was enough for one day. If the Louderbush-Stiver relationship soon became public knowledge, Mrs. Stiver would learn about it, and it would hit her hard. She was resilient, though — if you could call semi-denial and TV-shrink bromides resiliency.

I said, "Most of the information I have is that Greg was struggling to make a life for himself that eventually you would have been happy to know about. But that struggle was hard and complicated, and he had a ways to go. And you should know that others who knew him share your view that Greg didn't seem like someone who would take his own life. Other people have also told me about his strength of character and strength of purpose."

"So is it possible," she asked, leaning toward me, "that Greg's death was not suicide? That it was an accident somehow? Or even — I gives me the heebie-jeebies just to think about it — that Greg was murdered? Pushed off that SUNY building or something?"

I said, "An accidental fall from a SUNY roof seems unlikely.

Homicide is unlikely too, but of course not out of the question. All of that is what my client has me looking into." Now I bit the bullet. "In my attempt to gather as much information as I can on Greg and his life, I'm trying to talk to everyone who knew him. Would it be possible for me to ask your husband a few questions? I'll definitely try to avoid provoking him."

She slumped a bit. Then she looked at me closely. "What happened to your ear?"

"It's a rugby injury."

"Oh, that's too bad."

"You said your husband was busy, but I wouldn't take up very much of his time. I promise I'll be out of your family's hair in no time at all."

Was this really necessary? I knew it wasn't. I already had as clear an idea of Anson Stiver as I was likely to get short of psychoanalyzing the terrible man. Had he been beaten as a child, too? Probably. But all I really wanted was to form a firsthand impression of the beast who had set so much of this sad dysfunction — and worse — in motion, and here was my chance.

Mrs. Stiver said, "Anson is in the living room — it's his bedroom now — working on his transformers. He designs and builds miniature power transformers. But since his stroke last fall his speech is difficult to understand, and you might have a hard time getting what he's trying to say. Anyway, I wouldn't mention Greg to him if I were you. That would just set him off. And since his stroke, he's been forced to give up smoking. So Anson has been a bit hard to live with. I look after him as well as I can, and we have Filipino girls who come in three days a week. That's when I get to go out and do something I love to do."

"What's that, Mrs. Stiver?"

"I work in a daycare center. Lively Tots, in Amsterdam. I've always loved children, and people say I'm good with the kids, and they love me back."

She looked at me to gauge my reaction to this information, and I obliged by saying that that all sounded like a fine idea.

CHAPTER SEVENTEEN

Louderbush had not called back. I drove through the onrushing downpour back toward Albany, picking up my phone and putting it down more than twice, thinking maybe if I jiggled it, it would show a missed call from the assemblyman.

My visit with Anson Stiver had been brief and unhelpful in any important way. The retired engineer was slouched in his wheelchair, a portable oxygen unit at his side, his big frame a collapsed wreck. His speech, to the extent he had anything to say to me, wasn't just hard to understand; it was largely indecipherable. Was there a book? *When Bad Things Happen to Bad People.*

Stiver wasn't happy that I was not from Time Warner — a block of programming had gone out that included CNBC and the Fox Business channel — and he was even more put out when Mrs. Stiver introduced me, at my suggestion, as someone interested in establishing a kind of memorial for Greg. Stiver was immediately suspicious, and he seemed to be asking why it had taken five years for anyone to get around to this.

"His many friends have been so busy with their academic careers," I said. "But Greg's sad passing haunts us all."

He looked as if he wasn't going to buy that at all. He said something else I couldn't follow, but his hard gaze was on my bandaged ear, and I wasn't surprised when Mrs. Stiver said to him, "He hurt his ear playing rugby."

Stiver snorted at that and then made more noises that I couldn't make out and shook his head vehemently.

Mrs. Stiver translated this as, "If the memorial is some gay thing, no money. If it's not a gay thing, twenty-five dollars."

I told him it was a gay thing. I wanted to add *Give me the twenty-five dollars anyway or I'll break your nose,* but of course I didn't.

I left soon after.

I got Timmy on the phone. "Still no word from Louderbush.

But I've met Stiver's parents, and I can see how young Greg might have fallen into a self-destructive relationship with an older man." I described the unfortunate Margery Stiver and her hulking ruin of a bad-news husband.

"No surprises there, right? Did you learn anything at all?"

"No, but Stiver's mom is yet another character in this confused psychodrama who considered him a highly unlikely candidate for suicide. She said why would anybody tough enough to survive someone as awful as her husband then suddenly fall apart mentally in a situation where choices were available? She talked about how strong Greg had always been."

"Yes, but maybe that was the problem. Stiver knew he was a tough survivor, and yet here he was being worn down — physically even — by yet another violent man. And he couldn't find the courage to put an end to a situation he saw as humiliatingly self-destructive. He couldn't face going on that way. It wasn't who he thought he was and who he wanted to be."

"That's an entirely plausible summary. But the way Insinger and Jackman described Stiver's last weeks seemed to suggest some particular deterioration in Stiver's circumstances that he was having a bad time coping with. The teaching job situation or maybe some new disturbing wrinkle that Louderbush had introduced into the equation."

"I guess only Assemblyman Louderbush would know the answer to that question."

The rain was easing off now, and I could make out misty sunlight up ahead over the western outskirts of Albany. "I'm assuming Louderbush will call back soon. He obviously knows what I'm working on, and now he knows I know he knows, so he has to believe I'll eventually track him down on my own terms. And he'd rather we met on his."

"He should hurry up."

"I think he will. He definitely does not want any of this to become an election issue. Though how he can avoid it at this point beats me. The circumstantial case against him keeps building. One thing I'd like to know is, how come Louderbush's staff was making official inquiries out at SUNY about Stiver's suicide? Was Louderbush trying to scope out whether or not Stiver had mentioned Louderbush in a suicide note or elsewhere in an incriminating way? You don't happen to know anybody on Louderbush's staff, do you? I asked Tom Dunphy if he had a mole there and he didn't."

"I only know Louderbush's people very casually. There's somebody I could ask though. Ann Holmes dated a Louderbush staffer for a while. I think the guy she dated no longer works there, but he might remember something."

"Isn't Ann Holmes a Howard Dean fanatic? What was she doing dating somebody working for a reactionary like Louderbush?"

Timmy chortled. "Well, if you really need to know…"

"Know what?"

"This guy, Frogman Ying, was famous for his incredibly long tongue. He was a Taiwanese Chinese-American who sort of got passed around among Ann and her gang for a year or so."

"Frogman?"

"His real name was Alex."

"You think he's still in Albany?"

"I've seen him around. He works for the taxation committee as I recall. He could work magic with numbers, Ann said. But not *just* numbers."

I said, "Do straight women confide these sorts of things to their straight male friends or just their gay male friends?"

"Oh, I think you know the answer to that one. It's one of the ten reasons we were invented."

"What are the other nine?"

Timmy said he'd have to consult Walter Scott's *Personality Parade* for the answer to that, and meanwhile he'd try to track down the gifted Mr. Ying.

I decided that Louderbush had concluded that he didn't need the Serbians harassing me anymore and I could safely return home. Crow Street did feel cozy and secure when I found a parking spot with inches to spare and maneuvered deftly into it. One of the few useful things I had learned in high school was parallel parking — algebra is overrated as a key to the good life — and I never failed to whisper thanks to my old driver ed teacher, Mr. Galitsky, whenever I practiced this essential urban skill.

Timmy wasn't home. He phoned and said he was having brunch with his old friend Ann Holmes, and he had a call in to Alex Ying. Timmy was going to feel out Ying on his current opinions on Assemblyman Louderbush. If they were negative, he'd level with Ying about the physical abuse charges and ask about the Louderbush staff inquiries into the Stiver suicide. If Louderbush was one of Ying's political heroes, I said the story might be that Stiver's family was setting up a memorial scholarship in his name, and did Ying recall if Assemblyman Louderbush was acquainted with the late young conservative stalwart? If Ying said why not just call the office, Timmy would say it's Saturday and the office is closed and Ann Hoolmes suggested Timmy call Ying.

I checked my e-mails — nothing from Bud Giannopolous — and ate a bowl of Bola granola and put some coffee on.

My cell phone went off, and there it was again, Louderbush's number.

"This is Strachey."

"Yes. Mr. Strachey."

"I missed you last night. That Motel 6 set me back fifty-nine ninety-five. But let's try it again. I know you think this is as important as I do."

"Yes, I apologize. Anyone can tell you, missing appointments is out of character for me. But I had to deal with a situation before I spoke with you. I dealt with that situation, and now I'm clear going forward."

"Okay."

"I want to sit down with you and with one other person who is deeply affected by all this."

"All right."

"That other person is my wife."

What was this? "That sounds awkward."

He breathed heavily. "You have no idea."

"So she knows? About you and Greg Stiver?"

Another long pause. "Is this call being recorded?"

"No. If it was, I would be legally required to inform you of that fact."

I could all but see him rolling his eyes. "Yes, and I'm sure you're a law-abiding investigator, Mr. Strachey. Just like the law-abiding investigators who followed Eliot Spitzer into post offices and hotels."

"Yes, and I'm sure you're a law-abiding public official. Oh, thanks, by the way, for calling off the Serbians. They nearly ripped my ear off the first time I ran into them."

"I have no idea what you're referring to, and I have no need to know what your private eye snooping-into-people's-privacy type of life must be like. What I'm telling you is, I'm willing to meet with you, and when I told my wife, Deidre, what I was planning to do, she insisted on being there, too. I find this all just excruciating, and so does she. But she says rightly, I think, that her being there might help convince you and the people you are working with that what you are embarked on is just terribly wrong and unfair. And if you have any sense of justice — and of Christian charity, if I may say what's in my heart — then you and Tom Dunphy and Shy McCloskey will drop this entire wrongheaded line of investigation, and find something better to do with your time and your bushels of money."

"Wrongheaded in what way?"

"You'll see. Can you meet Tuesday morning? I'm at home in

Kurtzburg now and won't be back in Albany until Monday night. I have a friend who maintains a suite at the Crowne Plaza. Could you meet there?"

"I could drive out to where you are today or tomorrow. You're what, just west of Rochester?"

"No, don't come here. If you come here, it's no deal. I can't have someone like you being seen with me in my district. I'm sure you get that."

"Someone like me? Mr. Louderbush, can you hear yourself talking? If you did, you'd have to wonder."

More breathing. "I know what you think of me. And I admit some of it's deserved. But you don't know the whole story. Far from it. That's what you're going to hear on Tuesday, the whole story. And then you're going to think better of me. I promise you that you *will* think better of me."

It sounded like a con to me, and what I was mostly thinking about was the wire I'd wear and the additional evidence I'd end up with it that further revealed Louderbush's irredeemably rotten character.

We set the time and place for the Tuesday morning meeting, and I immediately called Timmy to update him on Louderbush's brazen gamesmanship. He was in the midst of his brunch with Ann Holmes and couldn't stay on the phone, but he said Frogman Ying had gotten back to him and was willing to meet me later that afternoon. Ying had told Timmy that Kenyon Louderbush was a great man who would make a great governor, and Ying was happy to hear that the Stiver family was setting up a memorial scholarship in Greg's name. He remembered Greg as one of a number of bright, promising young conservatives who had supported Assemblyman Louderbush and whose careers, academic and otherwise, had been boosted by the assemblyman. Greg was one of several college students who had been mentored by Louderbush. Greg was a particular favorite, but there had been others.

CHAPTER EIGHTEEN

"Who were the other college students Assemblyman Louderbush took an interest in?" I asked Ying. "Maybe some of them knew Greg and would like to participate in organizing the Stiver family's memorial scholarship?"

"I'm sure the assemblyman's office could give you a list. Why not just wait until Monday?"

"The family is interested in young conservatives who actually knew Greg. They'll be looking for donations, of course, but from people of your generation it's predominantly testimonials they're gathering. And doing it through you and others like you gives it all the personal touch the family yearns for."

Ying nodded and seemed to swallow this hooey. He was a slender Chinese-American youth of thirty or so with close-cropped hair and a single silver earring. Not your average Federalist Society Scalia-phile. Ying was just back from the gym when I met him in a coffee shop on Lark Street, so his tank top gave me a partial view of the fiery-tongued dragon tattoo that looped over a satiny beige shoulder and onto his right pectoral. He spoke with no discernible accent, and I wasn't surprised by his distinct enunciation. I caught myself watching his mouth opening and closing. Might I catch a glimpse of it?

He said, "I don't know that Greg had much contact with the other students the assemblyman mentored. They lived out in his district for the most part. In any case, Greg's situation was different. The assemblyman assisted Greg with his master's thesis, as I recall. That's what he told me after Greg died, and Mr. Louderbush asked me and another staffer to get hold of the SUNY report on the suicide. The assemblyman wanted to make sure the investigation was thorough and that the death was actually a suicide and not some sort of absurd accident the university was covering up."

"What did you find out?"

"That it was in fact a suicide. There was a note that the police found, and they notified the university."

"How well did you know Greg? His death must have come as a terrible shock. Or did it?"

"I liked him, but I didn't know him terribly well. He came into the office once for a tour, and I saw him occasionally at SUNY Federalist Society get-togethers. Have you talked to his rugby buddies? I don't know who they were, but I'm sure they'd be interested in the memorial."

"No, I haven't talked to them. I'd love to locate some of them."

"Ask the assemblyman. It's one of the interests he and Greg shared. It's a rough sport, too messy for a gym addict like me. But I know Mr. Louderbush played sometimes. Even at his age. He'd come into the office with scrapes and bruises. But he always said he found it invigorating."

"I know all about that."

"You play, too? Is that what happened to your ear?"

"Yep."

"Softball is rough enough for me. I grew up in Taipei and played Little League. My family moved to the US when I was twelve. Rugby was a bit exotic for me and my brothers."

"What's your favorite sport now?"

He laughed. "I'm tempted to say muff-diving, but I guess that's not what you were thinking about when you asked the question."

"Ha ha."

"Anyway, are you Timothy Callahan's friend? Why is a raving progressive like Timothy interested in a memorial for someone like Greg Stiver? Or is he a friend of the Stiver family? Or are you?"

"I am. Greg's sister, Jennifer, asked me to help out. This all goes beyond politics."

"Oh sure. It's one of the reasons I love this country. You can hold the most passionate ideological beliefs and still be friends with the opposition. It's one of the ways I disagree with the Tea Party types. They make it all too vehement and too personal. On the Supreme Court, Justice Scalia and Justice Ginsberg tear each other to pieces on the bench, and yet off the bench they're the best of friends. Take you and Timothy. You can disagree with Assemblyman Louderbush's positions, and yet you still respect him enough to want to memorialize an unfortunate young man who meant so much to him and to the conservative youth movement in Albany. What you're doing just serves to reaffirm my faith in my adopted country."

"Great."

"So are you supporting Shy McCloskey for governor? I gather you are."

"Timmy works for Myron Lipschutz. So, sure."

"It's not Shy's year. Four years ago maybe. But Kenyon Louderbush's time has come. He'll be a great governor. At a minimum, he'll keep New York State from turning into a basket case like California. Overspending, fiscal paralysis, government by the special interests — that's all over."

"You think Louderbush can really beat Merle Ostwind? New York has never elected anybody as far right as your former boss. Anyway, you don't go for the Tea Partiers' extreme partisanship. And yet they're Louderbush's main supporters."

"The assemblyman won't be dictated to by anybody. He's his own man. He's going to do what's right. He's not interested in Obama-hating and all that craziness — birthers and deathers and that crap. He simply wants to support and enable the capitalists that built this magnificent country and to let them work their magic the way they once did."

"Like in 1890? Before child-labor laws and food safety and minimum wage and any clean air or water laws at all?"

He smiled. "I'd go back even further than that. 1870?"

"Why stop there? Why not 1840 or 1850, when the US was a

virtual paradise?"

"Except for slavery and the cultural genocide of the Native Americans, sure, why not? Hey, you know what? I thought of somebody you should talk to about the scholarship fund. Randy Spong was a SUNY student who did his master's thesis on the Missouri Compromise and other ways the South fought politically to retain slavery. I remember him because he was in the Federalist Society for a while, and he came into the office once with the assemblyman. Randy was a year or so ahead of Greg, but I'm guessing they knew each other. As I recall, Randy was a rugby player, too."

"Any idea where Randy is now?"

"I think he's teaching at UVM. He was a couple of years ago, I know."

"The University of Vermont?"

"In Burlington."

"I'll try to track him down."

"I'm sure he'd like to help remember Greg."

"I'll be sure to get in touch."

Ying checked his watch. "I have to get going. I have a date — actually two dates." He grinned. "One at two and another one tonight. I promised my parents I'd be married by the time I was thirty. I'm twenty-eight, so I'm sowing my wild oats while I still can. They have a nice Chinese girl they want me to meet, and that'll be fine when it happens. But meanwhile it's gather ye rosebuds while ye may, if you know what I mean."

I said I thought I did.

CHAPTER NINETEEN

I asked Dunphy, "Does the campaign have an airplane I could use? I have to be in Hall Creek Monday morning and Burlington, Vermont Monday afternoon. I'm actually making some progress."

"We occasionally charter a plane for Shy, and we'll be doing a lot more of that as the campaign heats up. But do we have an aircraft standing by for your personal use? No, Strachey, we don't."

I told Dunphy about the possibility of other young men with whom Kenyon Louderbush had had abusive relationships and that I was trying to track down at least one of these people.

"Fantastic! That'd be the final nail in that asshole's coffin. Great work, Strachey. This is terrific!"

"I'm not there yet, but it's looking worse and worse for the assemblyman. Though here's a new twist, Tom. Louderbush has actually contacted me, and he wants to meet with me and his wife on Tuesday. He claims this is all just a misunderstanding, and once I hear his side of the story I'll report to you and McCloskey and we'll drop this whole opposition research operation. I think it's a crock, but I'm going to go ahead and hear him out. Can you get me wired up for the meeting?"

Dunphy whooped, "Holy shit, Strachey! Louderbush just called you up? That is incredible!"

"I was surprised, too."

"Oh my God, of course we can get you wired. Clean-Tech can probably do it. I'll check with them to see if they're equipped for that type of thing. Let me just run it by legal."

"Meanwhile, I can't be in two places at the same time. What's the air charter service you use? I'll set it up myself and bill you."

He fumed for another minute and then gave me a name and number. "I guess," he said, "after Kenyon falls by the wayside, the serious dough will start pouring in and the campaign will be able to afford you. But fuck, this had just better work."

"My thoughts exactly."

My semidetached ear was feeling more itchy than painful by now, but I went home and changed the dressing per my instructions from Albany Med. My headache was pretty much gone, and the atrocious hickey was fading away, too. My muscles were still achy, but I felt as though I could function more or less normally and would be ready to do what I had to in case the Serbians showed up again. I carried the gun in the chic shoulder bag with me at all times.

I got the air charter service on the phone and made arrangements for a Sunday night flight to the airport nearest to Hall Creek — it turned out to be Kurtzburg — and then a late-morning Monday flight up to Burlington, Vermont. Dunphy had already phoned the service and okayed the billing. I also asked for a rental car with a GPS at each location and a motel room in or near Hall Creek.

I e-mailed Bud Giannopolous and requested the name of someone in the human resources office at Hall Creek Community College. I said I also needed everything Giannapolous could come up with on a Randy Spong, who was on the faculty at UVM — or had been as recently as two years earlier.

Timmy came home, and we spent a couple of hours looking at *Humpy Mat Humpers* and wearing ourselves out in ways that were so much more enjoyable than my exertions on behalf of the Shy McCloskey gubernatorial campaign. I fantasized about Alex Ying's incredible long tongue and asked Timmy if he was doing the same. He said, "Eeww."

§ § § §

On Sunday, I updated and went over my notes, adding the names and data Bud Giannopolous had e-mailed me overnight. At five in the afternoon I drove out to Cavenaugh Air Service at Albany airport and was soon ushered out onto the tarmac and to the conveyance Dunphy had paid for. It was a three-seat single-engine Cessna piloted by a large florid man named Walt who took up most of the front two seats. I crouched in the single seat behind him and thought about Jesus. This flying *tuk-tuk* soon lifted off successfully and pitched about for two hours and fifteen minutes — I could see highway traffic down below moving only a little more slowly than we were — before oofing down onto the runway at Kurtzburg Municipal Airport. It was June and still light out, and I worried about running into Louderbush. But he was nowhere in sight among the business and recreational flyers I passed as I crawled out of my saltine tin and was led out to the rental car.

The motel the air service had booked me into — Walt would be putting up there also — was a locally owned relic called the Hall Creek Lodger Inne that advertised "color TV." The plumbing rattled as I unpacked my few belongings, and the fluorescent light in the bathroom buzzed like an alarm clock going off. But the place smelled of nothing worse than disinfectant, and after dining at the KFC down the road, I came back, read through the *Times* I'd brought along, and fell asleep. I dreamed yet again of the elegant blond woman jumping into San Francisco Bay.

The nice woman in the human resources office at HCCC, Melanie Fravel, asked me if I'd like some coffee, and I said thank you, I would. As I mentally rummaged through her files, she walked down the hall and came back shortly with a mug of coffee with the HCCC logo on it and two cinnamon buns, one for each of us.

"I can't recall that we ever had a visit from the FBI before now, so I have to tell you that this is a special occasion for us. I hope you won't be offended if I tell you that it's actually a bit creepy."

"Creepy? How so? Most special agents think of ourselves as workaday public servants."

Ms. Fravel went to work on her sweet bun, which from the looks of her was not her first of the day.

"It's not creepy because of you, but because this is the second time in — what? three days? — that someone from law enforcement has come asking about Gregory Stiver and his faculty appointment at HCCC five years ago."

"Really?" I chuckled knowingly. "Your tax dollars at work. What agency was my law enforcement colleague attached to, may I ask?"

I had shown her a badge I'd picked up at a security company uniform supply store on Suan Plu Road in Bangkok a few years earlier, and she hadn't taken notice of the Thai script on it.

"Well, he *said* he was with the Capitol Police in Albany."

"I'll check with them."

"I have to say that this gentleman didn't inspire trust and confidence the way you do, Mr. Strachey. He was more rough-hewn."

"Like some war criminal from the Balkans?"

"Oh, for heaven's sake, that's it exactly! You've described the gentleman to a T. Do you know him?"

"Possibly. What was his name? Do you recall?"

"John Jameson. He said he was Captain John Jameson. And that was the name on his ID. My goodness, could his credentials have been fraudulent?"

"I have no way of knowing. I'd have to examine them first hand or our lab would. What was Captain Jameson's interest in Greg Stiver and his faculty appointment?"

"The same as yours, if I understood your call this morning. He said Mr. Stiver's name had come up in an ongoing criminal investigation involving people still alive. Something about members of the state Assembly whose names had been used wrongly and without their knowledge to give candidates for state jobs a leg up? Is that it?"

"It is. I can see that the bureau needs to get its act together and coordinate better with other police agencies. I can't begin to tell you how embarrassed I am."

"Yes, isn't that how 9/11 happened? Poor coordination between agencies? I mean, I'm not blaming you."

"Well, we all share responsibility to some degree."

She ate some of her bun, and I had a chunk of mine.

She said, "In any case, there was certainly no misuse of our assemblyman's name in that regard. Mr. Louderbush personally called Mitch Darnell, our president, and endorsed Greg Stiver's faculty appointment. Not that any favoritism was involved. Faculty appointments are of course above politics. But we had a sudden opening for an associate professor of history and economics when one of our faculty resigned unexpectedly after her husband was transferred to Florida by his company. Mitch knew that Kenyon had this bright young man he'd previously mentioned to us. And all things being equal, Gregory Stiver filled the bill as well as anyone. We were all shocked and disappointed when Mr. Stiver died. And of course here at the college we were back to square one."

"Assemblyman Louderbush had no other candidate to offer?"

"Well, no. I don't think it was as if he had a cupboard full of young economists or anything."

"I'm reassured to hear this. It doesn't help our investigation particularly. But it certainly confirms my understanding that Mr. Louderbush's interest in Greg Stiver was genuine."

"I'm sure it was. Mitch said that when Mr. Louderbush personally called to inform him of Greg's suicide, the assemblyman was terribly distraught. He broke down, Mitch said, and was unable to complete the call. Suicide is so mysterious. It just goes against everything we believe about human existence when we get up in the morning. Do you have any idea why Greg killed himself? We never learned any more about him."

"That's outside the purview of the FBI. But I suppose Assemblyman Louderbush knows something about what happened. You might ask him the next time you see him."

CHAPTER TWENTY

The flight to Burlington took over four hours in our tricycle with a surfboard across it, and my breakfast cinnamon bun was restless in the bumpy air. I asked Walt to wait at the airport; I had tracked Randy Spong down at home with a cell number Bud Giannopolous had come up with, and Spong had agreed to see me if I promised to leave his apartment by four forty-five. I had told him I was investigating the circumstances surrounding Greg Stiver's suicide, including Kenyon Louderbush's possible involvement. This honesty seemed like the approach that would work best with him, and also I wasn't sure I could come up with any more appalling bald-faced lies that day — though in a pinch, for a higher cause, I of course could have.

Spong lived not far from the UVM campus in an apartment on the second floor of the carriage house behind a pretty old Victorian mansion that seemed to have gone either gay or Mexican: a yellow exterior with lavender trim. Either way, it was a beauty.

I climbed the outside wooden steps to the apartment, and I saw right away why Spong wanted me out of there by a quarter to five. The elfin young man was bruised and swollen, and five o'clock was probably when his abusive boyfriend came home from work. Spong was stringily muscular, but all his strength was in his arms. His eyes showed no durability at all. He was barefoot in shorts and a T-shirt that said I HEART TRANSYLVANIA. He had an angular face with a Roman nose and big brown eyes that would have been sexy if they hadn't been black and blue.

I said, "Thanks for talking to me about Greg. It looks as if you and he had something in common."

"You mean we were both economists?"

"Not just that."

He smiled weakly. "You're so perceptive."

He shoved some books and papers aside on the couch and sat down, and I sat in one of the old easy chairs in the room, though not the one that directly faced the TV set, which gave off a distinct aura of territoriality. The bookshelves on one wall were stuffed to overflowing, and the art posters on the walls were Franz Kline, Escher, and Lucy and Charlie and the football.

I said, "But you're not going to end up like Greg, I hope."

He shrugged. "Not really. If I really hated my life as much as you must think I do, I wouldn't end it. I would change it. And eventually I think I will. Just not yet."

"So you get some kind of satisfaction out of being abused by your boyfriend?"

"I wouldn't use the word *satisfaction*. It's more complicated than that. And I like complicated emotions. But, no, I'm not completely detached from reality. I know this is basically unhealthy. For me and for Serge."

"Serge. What is he, some kind of Russian bear? You could really get hurt, you know."

Another little smile. "Serge isn't Russian. He's Swiss. He's older than I am, and he's not much bigger than I am. I could strangle him if I needed to. But strangling Serge is not what I need. What I need is what you see."

"How do you explain it at work? The bruising and so on."

"I don't. People can think what they want to think. I'm very good in the classroom, so my position is secure. Occasionally a well-meaning colleague tiptoes up to the elephant in the room and asks me if they can help or if they can direct me to someone. I just say no thank you."

"I take it that in your personal history this all goes way back."

"Of course."

"You don't want to be free of that?"

"No, not yet."

I checked my watch. We had another hour.

I said, "Suppose Serge came back while I was here? How would he react?"

"Well, we're not going to test that supposition. But it wouldn't be pretty."

"Is he jealous?"

"You could put it that way. The other person in any of those situations is safe, however. You wouldn't have to be carrying a revolver in that bag you brought in in order to protect yourself. I would be the one who bore the brunt after you left."

"And that's what you want."

"I do need to take a day off sometimes. I've learned how to pace myself and stay out of the ERs. We don't want that."

"Did Kenyon Louderbush beat you?"

"Of course."

"He was your abusive lover?"

"For a year. Then Greg came along."

"So Louderbush trolled for boyfriends in SUNY econ classes? That's where you met him?"

"Kenyon never came to class, no. He was never that subtle. He cruised the men's room in the Performing Arts Center every week or so. I suppose that's where he met Greg, too."

"Did you resent Greg's replacing you in Louderbush's…is *affections* the word I want?"

"For a while. But it was time for me to move on anyway. And I knew Greg and wished him well."

"Were you in Albany when Greg died?"

"No, I'd moved up here in January. I heard about it from friends. I cried. Which I don't do very often. I learned a long time ago how not to."

"Some people who knew Greg think Louderbush somehow drove him to suicide."

A little sigh. "It doesn't work that way. Greg was a grown-up."

"But pretty unhappy, according to two neighbors of his. He was more ambivalent about the abusive relationship he was in than you are about yours."

"You think I'm not ambivalent?"

"I was getting the impression you find it fulfilling."

"Yes and no. That's called ambivalence, I believe."

"Okay."

"Anyway, Greg was not the type to commit suicide."

"There's a type?"

"I mean only that he had quite a muscular ego. He believed in his ideas and he believed in himself. The need to be abused was an important part of Greg's makeup — I assume it had to do with his home life growing up, though I really know nothing about that — but being kicked and hit was not central to his spiritual existence. There was plenty else about him that was sturdy in a conventional way. I really thought he would go on to be successful as a conservative writer and teacher — probably show up on Fox and maybe write speeches for people like Kenyon. That he would just throw all that away seemed so out of character. Greg was somebody who saw a future with him in it. But, as I say, I wasn't all that close to Greg, so maybe there were other demons I never knew about."

"What do you think of Louderbush's candidacy for governor?"

"I wish him Godspeed. Maybe he'll win and break the Senate Democratic leadership's nose. They've had it coming for years."

"I'm working for the Shy McCloskey campaign. We want to expose Louderbush as a closeted gay man who beats up his gay lovers and isn't fit to hold public office."

An eyebrow went up, though only just perceptibly. "I thought that might be what you were up to."

"Would you be willing to sign a statement describing your relationship with Louderbush, including the abuse?"

"Of course not."

"You don't see this history of his as a character flaw so serious that it precludes his being in charge of, say, state mental health programs?"

"What do you think a Governor Louderbush would do? Subsidize gay guys beating up their boyfriends? I wouldn't worry about that. Kenyon is a libertarian. He thinks government should mind its own business. And maybe you should, too."

"Did Louderbush have other gay lovers he abused besides you and Greg?"

"I believe so. He referred to someone occasionally out in his district. Some hot number he liked to get drunk and pound on. I'm sure there had been others. But even if I knew who these men were, I wouldn't provide you with their names. That would be presumptuous on my part."

I went round and round with Spong for another fifteen minutes — we both kept a close eye on our watches — but I finally had to accept the near certainty that he would be no help at all in exposing Louderbush. He had some highly theoretical idea in his head as to what it would be like to live normally, but it was so far outside his experience that he simply had no objection to anybody else's making intimate human connections primarily through violence.

At a quarter to five, I said, "You're looking apprehensive. I guess I had better get going."

"Thank you, yes. My pulse rate is up. I can actually feel my heart pounding in my chest. In a way, I wish you'd stick around. This is getting exciting. The dread is palpable."

There was no point to my telling him there were programs and yada yada. He knew all that. I thanked him and wished him well.

As I pulled out of the driveway in my rental car, an old Chevy Caprice drove by me, and in the mirror I saw it park in the spot I had just vacated in front of the carriage house. I kept on going.

CHAPTER TWENTY-ONE

Dunphy said, "Shy wants to meet you before you see Louderbush tomorrow. Can you work it out? I know this is last minute."

I'd just gotten into my car after the flight back from Burlington and had phoned Timmy and told him I was on my way home. It was just after eight, and I was looking forward to going out for a beer and a plate of something zesty.

"Yeah, sure. You mean now?"

"Have you eaten? There's a private dining room at Da Vinci."

"Give me twenty minutes."

"Make it fifteen."

I got Timmy back and told him that instead of joining him for dinner I'd be dining with the man who might be the next governor of New York, depending on how my meeting with Kenyon Louderbush went the next morning.

Timmy said, "You're a god. But be careful of your ear."

"It's good I have a spare."

"I doubt McCloskey will do much more than bend it. He's famous for that."

"Your boss has dealt with him. Any advice on how to approach McCloskey?"

"He's a fairly honest guy, and more or less straightforward. He's been known to put up with some dubious types on his staff, and I think he's not above *Do what you have to and don't tell me about it* kinds of operations. But nothing really outside the normal murky parameters of American political functioning. Also, he's a good liberal overall and a nice guy. Just be up front with him, and you two will hit it off."

"But aren't I one of those dubious types? Should I tell him stories about how I go about my business? Will he be charmed, or will he get up and run out of the room?"

"I wouldn't necessarily go into specifics."

"In the last couple of days I've impersonated a memorial scholarship organizer, a federal agent and a producer for BBC America. I shouldn't regale him? Old Irish pols love a good story."

"No. And whatever you do, don't say anything about Bud Giannopolous. Senator McCloskey mustn't know about him, and for that matter neither should Tom Dunphy. I'm certainly sorry *I* know more than I should about this criminal. I'm probably borderline culpable."

"I'm making a note." I thought, but didn't add, What I am dealing with here is a mild paranoiac educated by Jesuits.

Da Vinci was a relic of Old Albany, a downtown red sauce joint with frayed white linen and potted ferns where pols and judges once rubbed elbows with gangsters. The thugs had long since been replaced with the paid representatives of business and professional organizations who brandished not gats but checkbooks. A doddering maître d' led me past the scattering of occupied tables and through a doorway in the rear of the restaurant. Then he went out again, shutting the door behind him.

"Don Strachey, I've heard so much about you! We meet at last. What a pleasure."

Dunphy added, "Senator McCloskey has met private investigators before. But none, he was just telling me, with such a colorful history as yours, Don."

"Snoops all tend to be corporate types now," McCloskey said. "Not the racy independent operators that make up such an irresistible slice of bygone Americana."

"I'm pleased to meet you, Senator. I'm one anachronistic PI who's at your service."

McCloskey had risen as I entered the room and shook my hand. It may have been the ten millionth hand he had shaken, but his grip was confident and lingering. He was a good six-three with a comfortable paunch, a big mobile face and a stubble of late-day beard. He hadn't removed his jacket or loosened his necktie, and he projected both dignity and an easy camaraderie.

"You know, I've met Barney Frank," McCloskey said. "A bit cranky — doesn't suffer fools — but brilliant, brilliant. We've come a long way in this country since Walter Jenkins was forced to slink out of the LBJ White House for being gay. Not that Kenyon Louderbush isn't a very different sort of animal from people like you and the congressman from the Gay Peoples Republic of Massachusetts. But we'll get to that. What are you drinking, Don?"

We settled in, and Dunphy and McCloskey exchanged some gossip about their gubernatorial campaign as well as the two others. A waiter materialized with antipasti and soon was back with a Sam Adams for me and refills for McCloskey's and Dunphy's bourbons. McCloskey ordered a Caesar salad and a bowl of minestrone. Dunphy and I both put in for the linguini with clam sauce and the hemisphere of iceberg lettuce with blue cheese dressing.

"Normally," McCloskey said after the salads arrived and the door to our small room had been closed again, "anything as momentous as urging a political opponent to withdraw from a race would not be carried out by hired help such as yourself, Don. Matters this weighty — and this delicate — would be handled by senior staff or, failing that, if it came to it, via selected leaks to the *Times* and the *Post*."

"Or," Dunphy said, "via an anonymous bundle of photographic horrors somebody receives in the mail. Don't forget that time-honored variety of political malpractice."

McCloskey chuckled. "It's been known to happen. But this business with Kenyon," he went on, "is a whole 'nuther matter. It calls not just for the right balance of toughness and discretion. It requires a nuanced understanding of the special circumstances we're dealing with — the gay thing as well as the pathology. You're up to this, Don? Tom promises me you are."

"I'm not a psychologist, but I'm not sure that's necessary. I get the basics, and anyway what's called for here is mainly a healthy sense of outrage along with a working bullshit detector."

"Tom tells me Kenyon contacted you, and he thinks he can convince you that this whole investigation of ours is a load of crap."

"He did, and he does."

"How can he be so naive? You're convinced it's not crap, I take it."

"Oh, yes. I believe it. I'm still in the process of locating witnesses who are actually willing to testify to Louderbush's exploitive abusive practices. But as for myself, I'm more than convinced."

"What have you gotten in writing or on tape?"

"Nothing actually in affidavit form so far. One witness, a young man in Vermont who was also abused by Louderbush, won't help out; he's too much of a psychological mess himself. A young woman who Greg Stiver confided in works for a company where controversy is verboten, so she's reluctant to go public with what she knows. But a former boyfriend of the woman friend, Virgil Jackman, will testify. He's solid and he's credible."

"Tom tells me Jackman is the son of a former IUE shop steward?"

"He is."

"Okay. What else have we got?"

"Lots of circumstantial evidence. The police report on the Stiver suicide was doctored, apparently to delete references to inquiries by Louderbush's office. Unfortunately, the susceptible cop in charge is no longer with us."

"Retired to Sarasota?"

"Dead."

"Oh boy."

"But there's evidence at SUNY that Louderbush was making

odd inquiries about the death. What was his interest? A former Louderbush staffer says the assemblyman was a quote-unquote mentor to Stiver. But Louderbush's snooping seemed to go beyond mere sadness and loss. He seemed intent on finding out if his name came up in any context and if there was any doubt about the verdict of suicide."

"Jesus. Is it possible Louderbush actually *pushed* Stiver off the roof at SUNY? That this was a homicide?"

"Why do you ask?"

"That would be a good deal tidier than what you've told me so far. Make great headlines in the *Post* and the *Daily News.*"

"Well, it's not out of the question. One witness thinks she saw two people on the roof of the building before Stiver fell."

"One witness thinks… Not much there, I guess. But what about this violence against yourself, Don? Your head injury there. Tom says you're convinced that Kenyon is responsible, although I take it that so far you have no direct evidence of that. Jesus, I knew they played hardball in Kurtzburg, but this would be way out of bounds."

"Tom may also have mentioned that for the first several days of my investigation I was under close surveillance, possibly electronic, by unknown persons. I could barely scratch my ass without somebody noting the gesture for posterity. Also, some real or fake Capitol cop preceded me asking pointed questions out in Hall Creek, where Louderbush had gotten Stiver a job at the community college."

McCloskey screwed up his face. "Peculiar. Very peculiar. It sounds downright sinister. Though if Kenyon is behind any of that type of thing, I'd be surprised. His organizational skills have always been limited."

"Be assured, Senator, that I'll be bringing all this up tomorrow when I meet with Louderbush. I'll be gauging his reactions, and more importantly I'll be wearing a wire."

McCloskey all but fell off his chair. He raised both hands as if to ward off any more flying information. "Oh, no. I don't need to know that."

Dunphy said, "For chrissakes, Don, we'll work out the details of your meeting on our own. Shy just needs framework."

"It sounds," McCloskey said, "as if Kenyon is going to throw himself at our feet and beg for mercy and forgiveness. I'd almost like to be present, but my stomach isn't as strong as it once was. He's bringing his wife along?"

"That's what he told me. She's involved, he says."

"I'm sure she is. Tom, if you were going to discuss your most sordid affairs with a private investigator, would you bring Doreen along?"

"Oh sure."

"Joyce would rather stay home, would be my guess. But this is the age of the political wife who can't tell the difference between loyalty and masochism. You saw Silda Spitzer standing there next to her no-goodnik hubby taking it on the kisser in front of Gabe Pressman and the rest of the known media world. And what's-his-name from Jersey, the guv with the Israeli butt boy boyfriend. Hava Nagila! The man's poor wife stood there next to him grinning like she was at their little girl's ballet debut, and her husband is telling the cameras he prefers sucking dick to eating pussy. No offense intended, Don."

"None taken."

"What's the story with Kenyon's missus, Tom? Do we know anything about her?"

"She's a nurse. Stays out in Kurtzburg. That's about it. They have kids."

"Sure they do. Don, have you checked Kenyon's children for broken bones?"

"No. I don't think it usually works that way with Louderbush's type. It's one thing or another. With him, it's grown-up young men, and sex is part of it. Anyway, a nurse wouldn't put up with that."

"You're probably right."

"The wife, I think, will be there for moral support for Louderbush and to exact sympathy from us."

"Yeah, well, don't extend any on my behalf."

"Okay."

"I certainly wish you well in your endeavors tomorrow. I know you understand that the future well-being of the state of New York may well hinge on your giving Kenyon the shove into oblivion he so richly deserves. And, as a practical matter for yourself, if you succeed here you'll have the world at your feet, I promise you. The world may never know exactly *why* you are so highly regarded by the governor of New York and in the corridors of power throughout the Empire State. Our fervent hope, of course, is that Kenyon will plead a prior engagement and politely withdraw from the race and none of this nauseating garbage will ever see the light of day."

"That's my hope, too, Senator."

Dunphy said, "I think we've got the guy by the short hairs. Today's Monday. If Kenyon is still in the race Wednesday, I'll be surprised."

"Unless, of course," McCloskey said, "he denies everything and tells Don here that his evidence is laughably thin and we can all go to hell. Is that a possibility? Could it be we're moving too soon on this?"

Twenty-four hours later, I repeated to Timmy McCloskey's description of how everything might go wrong, and I told him, "If only what happened at the meeting with Louderbush had been that simple."

Chapter Twenty-two

I jogged the loop around Washington Park four times and was back home by seven thirty. Cool weather had set in along with a low cloud ceiling that felt more like a disappointing version of April. I showered as soon as Timmy was out of the bathroom, then read the *Times* online with my coffee and English muffin. He went out the door to walk to work, saying as he went, "As they say in Thailand, good luck to you, good luck to you, good luck to you."

I went over my notes until eight thirty when two Clean-Tech operatives, Rod and Eugene, arrived on schedule. The cool weather worked to their advantage as they wired me up. I had on khakis and a sports jacket over a nicely styled T-shirt of the type Anderson Cooper might wear to a famine. A minimally bulky device the size of an mp3 player fit in my breast pocket. Its microphone was a ballpoint pen in the same pocket. Plan B was a second ballpoint pen I would hold or place on a table with my notebook; it broadcast sound to a receiver in a nearby room at the hotel where another Clean-Tech op would be listening and recording.

At nine thirty I ambled outside and over to Washington Avenue and on down past the Capitol and Albany City Hall. The unseasonable chill only served to make me feel more alert. It took me back to high school football and the thrill in the air before a big game.

I reached the Crowne Plaza just before ten, on time, and rode an elevator to the twelfth floor. It occurred to me that Louderbush would have his own techies on hand to strip search me and remove the breast pocket device and maybe even the innocuous-looking ballpoint pen transmitter. But when he opened the door to the suite and he and his wife were apparently the only people present, I wondered why he was acting so confident.

"I'm Don Strachey."

"Kenyon Louderbush. This is my wife Deidre."

"Hello," she said, barely audible.

He was tense enough, but she was clenched all over and looked as if it was all she could do to contain her rage. He was tall and broad, an aging but still formidable right tackle. He had a big jaw and big hands and wore gentlemanly specs, his only visible concession to the passage of time. She was good-sized, too, stocky as opposed to stout, also a onetime athlete maybe. She had a round pretty face with a minimum of makeup and some big but not comically big hair tinted auburn and recently styled. Both of the Louderbushes wore the kinds of conservatively presentable outfits you'd expect a state assemblyman and his spouse to turn up in at a Rotary Club dinner back in his district. One of my thoughts was, am I underdressed for this occasion?

We arrayed ourselves around a coffee table where the hotel had thought to provide some fresh gladiola that were tall enough to obstruct Mrs. Louderbush's view of me. Without a word, she got up and transferred the vase to an out of the way end table. There were nuts and wrapped hard candies too, but nobody reached for any. There weren't of course any ashtrays.

"This is going to be painful for all of us," Louderbush said, "so let's get it over with."

Painful for all of us? "Sure," I said.

"I called you, Mr. Strachey, because I've had reports coming in that you are on my case for some immoral things I did many years ago."

"Five years ago is not many years ago," I corrected him.

"No, not to you it isn't. But to me five years ago is another lifetime."

"Well, you did what you did. Repeatedly over a number of years apparently."

"I can't deny that. I'm not here to deny anything. I'm here to...try to get you to understand what some of the consequences will be if you and Shy McCloskey make my sins of the past a campaign issue."

"Consequences for whom?"

"I'll get to that. Primarily for my family." Mrs. Louderbush tightened up even more and was glaring up a storm. She had set down a shoulder bag that was even bigger than mine — both rested on the end table separated by the gladiola — and I hoped she didn't also have a weapon in hers.

"Deidre and I have three teenage children," Louderbush went on. "This is an extremely vulnerable age. Teenagers are so sensitive, so easily hurt and confused. They need their parents. They need to be able to look up to their parents."

"No, I'd hate to see any young people get hurt. I mean, any more than have been injured already."

Mrs. Louderbush looked at her husband and started to say something, but he shook his head. "You're going to be merciless with me," he said, "and I understand why. Believe me, I do. I've been in counseling since Greg Stiver's death, and I can tell you that nobody is as angry at me as I am at myself."

"Good."

"I don't think I need to relate to you the whole dreary story of my upbringing and my life with my violent father and my being raped by my uncle Alan when I was twelve and all the rest of an incredibly sordid tale. But my young life made me a psychological cripple of the worst kind, the kind of man who preys on younger men who have been made vulnerable by family traumas of their own. I can't justify anything I have done. I can only explain. And I can say over and over and over again that I am so, so, so sorry for all the pain I inflicted, and I can honestly declare that I am beyond all of that horror. And, yes. It was Greg Stiver's death that forced me to confront my demons and my anger-management problems and to seek help and to promise myself and my wife that I would never enter into one of these sick relationships ever again. I also quit drinking, which had been a factor in my behavior."

Mrs. Louderbush said levelly, "It's true. It's all over."

"You knew about it?"

"Of course not!"

"No, no," Louderbush said. "I was a sneak. I was a liar and a sneak."

Now she was nodding angrily.

"It wasn't the illicit relationships that Deidre found out about. I have to say I covered my tracks too well to get caught at any of that. No, it was the therapy twice a week in Rochester. I was so faithful about my appointments that I began making up stories about my unexplained absences from my district office and from home. After a while, Deidre confronted me. What she thought was, I was having an affair."

"With a woman," she said coldly. "I'm a nurse, and you wouldn't think I'd be quite so naive."

"When did you find out about your husband's physically abusive relationships with young men?" I asked her. I wanted to make certain we were all talking about the same thing here.

"In January. The first thing I did was tell Kenyon I still loved him and I was not going to break up our family. The second thing I did was go out and get an HIV test. Fortunately, it was negative."

"This past January? Wasn't that when you announced you were running for governor, Assemblyman?"

"That was something of a coincidence and something of a not-exactly-a-coincidence. In any case, I planned on informing Deidre of my problematical past. I chose to tell her because she deserved to know — and just in case during the gubernatorial campaign certain types turned up."

"Gotcha. Certain types like me."

"Exactly."

"And by then you must have had your Serbians standing by to deal with any such crude interference with your plans, no?"

"Serbians?"

"I call them that. The goons that you — or more likely low-lifes on your staff — employed to try to intimidate me. My health insurance covers my damaged ear. Otherwise I'd send your campaign the hospital bill."

He stiffened. "That's ridiculous."

Mrs. Louderbush looked even madder.

"Mr. Louderbush, if you don't know this, you should. Since I've been investigating your ugly past, I've been beaten and my car has been vandalized. My movements have been monitored as if I was a sex offender wearing an ankle bracelet. Which strikes me as hugely ironic, now that I think about it."

Louderbush winced. "No. None of that is any responsibility of mine. Not this time. I'm sure in your line of work you've made one hell of a lot of enemies. Maybe you should go over your professional digging-up-dirt-on-people files to see who else doesn't like you and what you're doing. As for me and any Serbians, so-called, I'm not that ruthless and I'm not that well-organized."

"You have a history of both."

"Can you show me any evidence you have connecting me to any such BS? I have a lot to atone for, but having my political opponents' henchmen attacked is not one of them. You're just way off the mark on this one, my friend."

I knew it was possible he really had been told nothing of the ugly stuff being done on his behalf. Rogue staffers could be behind it, or even fringe Tea Partiers who wanted Louderbush elected and were operating independently. But with his record as an accomplished liar, it was impossible to know which. I was certain, though, that whoever had been all over me for days and was determined to scare me off had been operating at a level of sophistication beyond the normal means of Second Amendment loonies and anti-tax hysterics in Minute Man costumes.

I said, "Whatever you know or don't know about the way I've been roughed up, Mr. Louderbush, the basic facts here are indisputable. You did a lot of bad stuff that's cruel and illegal and disgusting, and if the electorate found out about it, they would say no to your candidacy. Some would congratulate you on getting a grip and halting your destructive practices, and they would wish you well in your future private life. But most would not want to take a chance on you as governor. I know I don't. What you did to Greg Stiver is unforgiveable. If the voters knew about it, most of them would not forgive you either."

Louderbush reddened and slumped in his chair. "I was trying to help him," he said.

Mrs. Louderbush looked away.

"What do you mean, help him?"

"I was there."

"Where?"

"It was an accident."

"Greg's fall from the roof at SUNY?"

"I had tried to end the relationship. I was so guilt-ridden. I helped Greg find a teaching job near Kurtzburg — he hadn't had any luck on his own — and then I was overcome with…guilt. It was so close to home, and to my family, who mean everything to me."

"Were you overcome with guilt, or were you overcome with fear that you'd get caught?"

"All right, yes, both."

Mrs. Louderbush looked as if she wanted to get down on her hands and knees and crawl out of the room, but she sat there three feet from her husband, her angry gaze fixed on the gladiola.

"What happened?" I said.

"I called Greg and told him I needed to talk to him. He was at the SUNY library, and he agreed to meet me in an empty econ classroom on the eighth floor of Livingston Quad Four."

"Okay."

"We met, and we talked, and he was very, very angry with me. He said I was teasing him, setting him up a few miles from where

I lived and then refusing to continue the relationship. He said I was torturing him."

"Funny choice of words."

Louderbush bristled. "Do you want to hear the truth or not?"

"Go ahead."

"Greg began to cry. I couldn't console him. I tried to hold him, but he shoved me away and grabbed his backpack and ran out of the room. I followed him, and when the elevator didn't arrive immediately, he ran into a stairwell. I think he heard voices down below, so instead of running down the stairs, he ran up. I followed him and suddenly we were somehow on the roof. He walked around and around weeping, and just to get him down off there I said I would reconsider ending the relationship. I admit I didn't mean it, but Greg was just so desperate and out of control. We were near the edge of the roof. There was no railing of any kind. And when I moved toward Greg to lead him by the hand away from the edge, he dropped his backpack and was turning toward me when he lost his balance somehow — he was sobbing and completely dazed and distraught — and he fell backward over the edge. Suddenly he just wasn't there anymore."

I thought, He's seen *Vertigo*. Does an old nun appear behind him at this point and make the sign of the cross?

"Mixed with my horror," Louderbush went on, "was my fear that someone might have seen Greg and me on the roof and would think that we were fighting and that I had pushed him to his death."

"Mm."

"I couldn't see anyone who might have observed us, so I took the elevator down and left the building and headed toward my car as fast as I could without being conspicuous."

"Did it occur to you that Greg might be alive and he would need help?"

"After a fall from that height? That would have been impossible."

"Maybe."

"I knew it would look like suicide — why else would he have gone up to the roof? — and I drove to Greg's apartment to fake a suicide note. I had a letter he had once written to me at a time when *he* had decided to end the relationship. He had written in big letters at the end of the note *I hurt too much.* I had the letter with me — I wanted to show it to Greg and remind him that the relationship was as painful and difficult and unrealistic for him as it was for me — and I ripped off that line and left it on Greg's desk. His friends found it there, and even the police were convinced that Greg's death was a suicide."

"Yes, they were. And your office snooped around SUNY and the Albany cops trying to find out if anybody had any suspicions regarding the verdict."

"You know that already."

"I do."

"And were there suspicions?"

"Some. But an Albany cop who didn't want any political high mucky-mucks involved in something dubious or messy saw to it that the case was closed and the suicide verdict certified."

"I was incredibly lucky."

"You bet you were."

"I drove back to my office. I mean I assume I drove there. I actually have no memory of it. I went into my office and cleared my schedule, and I sent my staff home. And then I got down on my knees and I prayed to God for forgiveness."

Here we go. "And were you forgiven?"

"That's a question I won't have an answer to until the day I meet my maker. But I went into therapy the next week, and now I have the kind of understanding of myself that makes it possible for me to control my impulses. And they *are* under control, as Deidre can attest to."

"How would she know?"

"I can read my husband," Mrs. Louderbush said. "I've lived with the man for twenty-six years."

"You didn't read him very successfully before last January."

"That's not true, not that it's any of your bleeping business. I sensed something was gnawing at him. I just assumed it had to do with his troubled childhood. Kenyon had always been moody because of that. If you'd ever met his father, you'd understand."

"And now he's a man at peace with himself?"

"More or less, yes, he is. Not of course taking into account the stress of the gubernatorial campaign and from having to put up with people of your ilk."

"Who's your therapist in Rochester?" I asked Louderbush.

"You know I can't tell you that. Or if I did tell you, my doctor would certainly not respond to any inquiries you might make."

"He or she might talk to me if I have some kind of waiver from you."

An incredulous shake of the head. "Forget it."

What was Louderbush doing? Was he being utterly honest and sincere, telling some reasonable facsimile of the truth even? And did he believe deep in his heart that I — and the McCloskey campaign — should accept his melodramatic tale on its face, and with a mixture of compassion for him and his family, as well as a belief in Christian redemption, simply drop the whole matter of questioning his fitness for office? Or was he, as I suspected, a pathological liar who had made up most or even all of the version of events he had just laid out for me so cogently, so tidily — too tidily, I was inclined to think.

I said, "Look, Mr. Louderbush, even if the McCloskey campaign agreed to overlook your past depredations, somebody else is bound to come along and get wind of this reeking stuff. I mean, I know about Greg Stiver and about Randy Spong, but how many other of these relationships were there?"

"A few."

"A few. Well, it looks to me as if you might be facing broken-nosed-college-boy eruptions throughout the general election campaign and, if you managed to beat Merle Ostwind and were somehow elected, well into a governorship you'd then be forced to resign from."

"No," he said firmly. "No one I was involved with would ever turn on me that way. They all respected me — even adored me."

His wife was looking a little queasy now, but she kept her mouth clamped shut. I thought of Frogman Ying, but I supposed Louderbush was referring to his resplendent conservative ideology and principles.

"You underestimate confidential anecdotal slippage. I first learned about you from two friends of Greg Stiver who he confided in."

Louderbush glanced at his wife and then looked at me evenly. "If any stories did begin to surface, it would help if the McCloskey campaign announced to the press that they had taken a close look at these ugly rumors, and Shy McCloskey has concluded that they are vicious slurs that have no basis in fact."

"I'm not following you. How could we possibly say that?"

He looked at his wife again, and this time she reached over and picked up her handbag. She reached into it. Was she going to bring out a pistol? No. It was a fat envelope.

CHAPTER TWENTY-THREE

The first name that leaped out was Nicholas Giannopolous. *Blabbedy-blah* Nicholas Giannopolous this, *blabbedy-blah* Nicholas Giannopolous that. Nicholas Giannopolous illegal penetrations of computer systems at the State University of New York at Albany; Nicholas Giannopolous illegal hacking of confidential files at Shenango Life Insurance Company; Nicholas Giannopolous illegal privacy violations of personnel records at Burton Hendricks Elementary School, Rotterdam, New York. What an accomplished technician Bud was!

Then my name started appearing. Donald Strachey impersonating a collector of funds for a scholarship in memory of deceased SUNY student Gregory Stiver; Donald Strachey impersonating a representative of the British Broadcasting Corporation in order to gain entrée at SUNY and procure private university information under false pretenses; Donald Strachey impersonating a special agent of the Federal Bureau of Investigation in order to obtain confidential personnel information at Hall Creek Community College, Hall Creek, New York.

Then fifty or sixty pages of transcripts of telephone conversations between me and Timmy, me and Bud Giannopolous, me and Jenny Stiver, me and my pal at APD, me and Millicent Blessing's secretary, me and Tom Dunphy, among others.

I flipped through the pages and now understood that my car had not been wired, and my computer had not been penetrated. It was my cell phone. My cell had been hacked.

I said, "Where did you get this stuff, Mr. Louderbush?"

"It was shoved through the mail slot at my home in Kurtzburg last night. There were two other copies besides this one. One is safely stowed away. The other I had sent by courier half an hour ago to Tom Dunphy."

His wife watched me with contemptuous eyes.

"Any idea who gathered this all up?"

"None whatsoever. Do you?"

"None offhand."

"It's quite a bundle for an ambitious federal prosecutor to sink his teeth into," Louderbush said. "A federal prosecutor or a reporter from the *Times* or the *Times Union* who's interested in illegality and corruption over at the Shy McCloskey gubernatorial campaign. It looks to me as if there's Pulitzer Prize potential here."

"It's all pretty innocuous, really."

"Impersonating a federal agent?"

"It's not treasonable in this case, although the law does frown on it."

"And are you recording our conversation as we speak, Mr. Strachey?"

"I might be."

"Ah. I might be, too."

I noted that the missus's handbag was aimed right at me.

"So, is it safe to say," Louderbush went on, "that we have arrived at a point of stalemate?"

§ § § §

My impulse was to call Timmy, but when I felt for my phone the thing seemed toxic in my pocket and I let go of it. I couldn't call Dunphy either. As I walked up State Street, the phone sounded its fluty little tune. I saw that it was Dunphy calling me; he must have received a report from the Clean-Tech listeners, and he would be instructing me to fly to Brazil for an extended period. I tossed the phone in a trash barrel in front of City Hall, then thought better of that and reached in and retrieved it. Bud Giannopolous would want to have a look at it.

I made it to Crow Street, not panicky but hyperalert, and picked up my car. I remembered vaguely where Giannopolous lived, in an attic in the Pine Hills section of Albany, ten minutes away. The big frame houses looked a lot alike on Giannopolous's street, but I was able to pick out his place from the wire antennas and satellite dishes on the roof. His building looked like a CIA safe house in Bethesda.

I would have been followed, but I didn't care. Somebody already knew about Bud, and about me as a client of Bud's, so what were they going to do next, say *boo*?

I parked the car on the street and buzzed Bud's intercom.

"Yo."

"Strachey."

"Abandon hope all ye who enter here."

"You're telling me."

The door clicked open, and I climbed the two wheezing flights. Somebody on the second floor had been smoking pot for breakfast and I took a deep breath.

Bud had a headset on when he opened his door, and I said, "Houston, we have a problem."

He gave me a little oh-no-bother wave of the hand as I stepped into a room that was piled high with Bud's poli-sci and world affairs book collection on one wall and a long table heaped with computers and other electronic gear against another. A dormer window looked down on the backyard of the house next door, where a man had a motorbike upside down and was fiddling with its front wheel. A poster on the rear wall of Bud's room showed a picture of some pita bread and a bowl of dip and bore the words *I am hummus, nothing is alien to me.*

"Can I speak freely in here?" I asked him.

"If not here, where?"

Bud was roughly five-feet-two and bore a striking resemblance to the one-time emperor of Ethiopia, Haile Selassie: ginger-skinned, high forehead, noble brow. Both Bud's bearing and his costume were more casual. He wore no medals and bore no scepter, and his outfit was non-imperial: ripped jeans, flip-flops, a faded T-shirt with an image on it of a squid wearing a hat that looked like a satellite dish. Nor would a crown sit easily on Bud's spiky little dreads.

"We may need lawyers," I said. "Or at the very least PR firms."

"Nah. What's up?"

"My cell phone was hacked."

He seated himself on his throne, an oversized wheeled office chair with cracked plastic armrests, and I perched on a bench. Stacked next to me were hundreds of techie magazines and computer catalogs, and the piles shifted ominously as I brushed against them.

"Not a big deal getting into cell phones," he said. "I've done it. All you need is an asset at whichever phone company it is who will give you the PIN code for anybody's phone."

"I guess this is against the law?"

He chuckled. "I would certainly hope so. What are we here, freakin' Hamas?"

"Well, in this instance there may be consequences — have been already." I retrieved the envelope from the Price Chopper supermarket bag the Louderbushes had provided for me and watched while Bud read through the transcripts and other documents.

"Holy Moly."

"Yeah."

"This is the product of a consummate professional."

"Do you recognize a professional colleague's work signature?"

"Well, no. It's not that easy. I'd need more samples, and I'd need to study them over time."

"I'll have to have a new phone, I guess. And number."

"I can fix you up."

"Are you and I going to go to prison, Bud?"

"Ha ha ha!"

Why was I not reassured? "I guess you can see from the

transcripts what I've been working on. The Shy McCloskey campaign hired me to prove that Kenyon Louderbush has had abusive sexual relationships with young men. This information — it's true, by the way — is supposed to drive him out of the gubernatorial race. I just met with Louderbush and his wife, and they handed me this bundle. They now consider me — and the McCloskey campaign — neutralized."

"Wow."

"So I'm in a bit of a pickle. I haven't talked to the McCloskey people about it yet."

"Kenyon Louderbush. My respect for that sorry old right-wing hack just went up."

"Not for his mixing sex with violence."

"No, that's creepy and disgusting. But I'm impressed as shit with his technical abilities — or somebody's. Any idea who did this stuff for him? It's ballsy and it's state of the art."

"I thought you said anybody could do it with inside technical data from a phone company. Verizon in my case."

"That's the easy part. It's doing it without the account holder becoming suspicious that's tougher. You haven't had any dropped calls or heard any weird beeps or clicks lately?"

"None that I noticed."

"Very nice work on somebody's part."

"Louderbush doesn't know who did it. This appalling packet was sent to him anonymously. Or so he claims. He could be lying. He's an experienced liar."

"This other hodge-podge of stuff — people you misrepresented yourself to in person supposedly. Can't you backtrack and find out who they talked to about you? It obviously wasn't law enforcement, or you would have heard from the feds by now, or at a minimum the attorney general's folks. Impersonating a BBC representative — that's a good one. I'll have to remember that. Can you do Telemundo?"

"I plan to backtrack, yes, and find out what I can. But now my cover is blown with these people — or some of them. It's hard to tell how many of my misdeeds were gleaned from the hacked phone calls and how many from interviewees ratting me out."

"Meanwhile, how can I be of assistance?"

"Can you hack into Louderbush's phone calls?"

"I can try. It may depend on which phone company he uses."

"I want to know who he's talked to in the past week and, if possible, what was said."

"Who he talked to, sure. Otherwise I can only get you voice mails. If you're talking about the next two weeks, I can maybe do better."

"Do what you can. Thank you."

A loud bang rattled the house, and then we heard a low *whoosh*.

"What's that?"

"The guy next door works on motor bikes in his yard. I hope he's all right."

We looked out the window, and the motorbike repairman was fine — and trotting through an open gate and out toward the street.

I followed Bud down the stairs and out the front door. My car was ablaze, the flames rising high and licking the lower branches of a handsome maple tree, with oily black smoke billowing and a frightful stench spreading across the neighborhood.

CHAPTER TWENTY-FOUR

The fire department found it puzzling. They doubted my story about having not tended to a fuel leak, although one fireman complained that Toyota wasn't the brand it once was. Anyway, one fireman said, the blaze seemed to have originated in the rear of the car near the gas tank. Two cops came by, acting mildly interested, and when the opinionated fireman told them it looked to him as if it could have been arson, one of the cops said to me, "Do you have any outstanding gambling debts, sir?"

I called a cab to take me downtown, where I rented another car. Bud had outfitted me with a fresh cell phone, having transferred the memory from my old one. The account holder on the new phone was his cousin Ephram. Bud kept the old phone and said he wanted to run some tests on it.

I assumed I was being watched — by multiple parties? — but I barged right into McCloskey campaign headquarters, Mr. Nonchalant. The multicultural young Phi Beta Kappas in the outer office didn't gasp or even look up, and I could see Dunphy in his office behind his desk.

"Holy shit, Strachey. Get in here and shut the door."

"Have you talked to McCloskey about what happened?"

"He wasn't stunned to hear about it. He had some choice descriptions of you. Loose cannon. Royal fuck up. Goddamn blithering gay caballero. Those are the appellations that are repeatable."

"I'm no longer an example of a bygone piece of colorfully beloved Americana?"

"He didn't mention that this time."

"Who does he think is behind this?"

"Merle Ostwind."

"That nice Republican country club lady? Come on."

"Not her personally. People who want her elected. Karl Rove? Rupert Murdoch?"

"So, this is all to protect Louderbush and keep him in the race. Then he trounces Shy in the primary and the freaked-out, mild-mannered New York electorate falls in behind Merle in the general. We're back to that scenario?"

"Did we ever leave it? If so, I missed that."

"How adept is Mrs. Ostwind with a gasoline-soaked rag and a match? Somebody just blew up my car."

He sat up. "No."

"Over in Pine Hills."

"Jesus, were you in it?"

"Do I look charred?"

"Oh my God. Are the cops on it?"

"Not in any serious way. Anyway, your name never came up. Or McCloskey's."

"I don't know what to say. God, I'm so sorry, Don. But I don't get it. If you've already been knocked out of the game by Louderbush's despicable blackmail, why would anybody do such a thing? Could it be something else you're involved in?"

"I think not something else, no. I assume it's the Serbians again. Whoever they are."

"More Serbians. Jesus."

"So, am I still on your payroll?"

"I was going to bring that up. Yes and no. Shy thinks we need to put a bit of distance between you and the campaign. All this impersonating a federal agent crap and the rest of it has given us all the heebie-jeebies. On the other hand, the senator doesn't want you turning into some embittered ex-employee going off half-cocked. Showing up on *60 Minutes* with a paper bag over your head and describing Shy and me as a reeking cesspool of political corruption, et cetera, et cetera. Also, Shy feels that you're the one who enabled Louderbush to blackmail us in the first place, and he'd like to give you the opportunity to get right with the Lord by blackmailing — I use that term facetiously, of course — by blackmailing Louderbush right back. If you can manage it this time."

"Isn't that how this all started out?"

"Blackmail isn't the word I would actually have used for threatening to expose a man's sadistic criminal activities. I'd call it law enforcement by other means. Karmic retribution? And of course it's all been in the interest of the higher cause of saving New York State from a bunch of Republican idiots."

"The only way out of this that I can think of is, I take the incriminating material I have on Louderbush and find somebody else to confirm it independently — a *Times* reporter? The *National Inquirer*? — and then step aside. Louderbush will blame me, of course, and McCloskey will have to disown me — your spokesperson will say I approached you guys with this odiferous stuff and you all told me to take a hike."

"I couldn't have put it more succinctly. This is exactly the approach we were going to suggest. Indirection. And publicly we disown you as seedy PI scum."

"Plus, all the risk will be mine."

"But you'll still be paid. Though from a special fund — an investigative journalism fund set up by a few of Shy's supporters."

"Oh, it's journalism now."

"Will the muck you've raked get in the papers? I should certainly hope so."

I thought, I'm in over my head. It had been a sense of liberal civic duty along with outrage over Louderbush's cruelty along with morbid curiosity along with the need to make a buck along with a comically exaggerated sense of self-importance that had gotten me mixed up in this sociopolitical-twisted-personality phantasmagoria in the first place. But there was still so much I didn't understand about any of it, and it all felt so fraught — would my next car explode with me inside it? — that I considered for about thirty seconds saying to hell with the whole thing.

Then it hit me that that's exactly what somebody wanted me to do at this point: quit. It felt all of a sudden that from the very beginning, I had reacted exactly the way somebody had wanted me to. The more I got roughed up — but never seriously injured — the more determined I had become, and that suited somebody just fine. Under the guise of warning me off, somebody who knew who I was, was egging me on. Somebody wanted an impasse between the McCloskey and Louderbush campaigns — but an impasse that could collapse at some third party's whim. A couple of carefully placed phone calls to reporters on spying, dirty tricks and corruption at the McCloskey campaign, along with a couple of carefully placed phone calls to *other* reporters on Greg Stiver's suicide and Kenyon Louderbush's involvement in it, would tip the election instantly to Merle Ostwind and the Republicans. It was all about timing.

So partly out of political loyalty, and partly out of a sense of injured pride and the need to get even, and partly out of a need to *understand* a set of circumstances that I knew was ultimately understandable, and partly out of the conviction that this unknown mendacious third party might also be neutralized or even exposed and sent to jail alongside Bud Giannopolous and me, I decided to stay in it. I now knew that all I had to do was look back at the way I had been manipulated and follow the motives.

CHAPTER TWENTY-FIVE

"What phone are you calling from?" Timmy said. "I almost didn't answer the call."

"My phone was hacked. That's how my movements were being monitored. I'd tell you or other people where I was or where I was going, and then when I got somewhere I was kept under surveillance — or beat up or my tires slashed. I'm using another phone somebody lent me. So make a note of the number."

"That's appalling. Is Louderbush behind it? I thought this was the big day. When you met him and convinced him to drop out of the race."

"I'm at the house. The confrontation with Louderbush didn't go well. What happened was, I tried to blackmail him — I'm using the term in the jocular sense the campaign likes to employ — and he blackmailed me right back. Louderbush and his little wifey."

"What? He threatened to expose you as a homosexual? How are you blackmailable?"

"He knew about Bud."

He collected his thoughts. "Well. Mister penitentiary-bound Giannopolous."

"Somebody tipped Louderbush off. Though tipped off may be too limited a term." I described the packet of materials that had been shoved through Louderbush's mail slot. "This stuff was dropped off at his house in Kurtzburg anonymously — or so Louderbush said. We know he lies through his teeth. He told me some wild story about being present when Stiver went off the roof at SUNY, and it was all just an accident, and now the assemblyman has put his unfortunate habits behind him, and we should all just leave him alone."

"Good grief. And his wife was there when he told you this story?"

"She was aiming a microphone at me apparently. All I had with me was a lethal weapon."

"Good for you for not using it."

"So, now I'm semidetached from the campaign and reduced to trying to find somebody else who's unblackmailable to drive Louderbush out of the governor's race, and I have to save my own ass to the extent that I am able. Also, somebody set my car on fire."

"But not your hair."

"I'm serious. The car was parked in front of Bud's place in Pine Hills, and while I was inside the Toyota went up in flames."

I could hear his head wagging. "You should quit."

"Nope."

"I'm frightened."

"So am I."

"This can't be the Republicans. It's somebody worse. The mob."

"Not likely, but it could be some Gordon Liddy type on the fringes of the party. A psychotic true believer. If so, it's a psychotic true believer with resources. But I've got resources, too. I've got the goods on Louderbush, and I've got Bud."

"Oh, wonderful."

I told Timmy I'd be in touch but that I might be spending another night away from home.

"How's your ear doing? And your hickey?"

"My ear just itches a little, and my hickey is now a pale aquamarine, barely disfiguring at all. When this is over, I want a fresh one, though not from the Serbians."

"I'm sure you'll be able to find someone in the federal pen at Danbury who can fix you up."

§ § § §

I called my car insurance company and gave them the info

on where the Toyota had been hauled off to. They would receive the police report, and I hoped they didn't deny me coverage on the grounds that my car had been destroyed on account of my unpaid gambling debts.

I got Bud on the phone he gave me, which presumably was secure. "Everything okay in Pine Hills?"

"I have Ephram and a few colleagues in the trade out here, and we're doing some security work on my systems. I got seriously hacked, and now walls are going up. It won't happen again. One of Ephram's more butch pals is down front keeping an eye on the front door. I'm cool. I'm also making some discreet inquiries as to who among the fraternity might have been working on the other side in this — whoever the other side turns out to be."

"That's exactly what I need to know. Who the other side is."

"Let me get back to you on that. We're all dying of curiosity."

I tracked down Frogman Ying at the state assembly taxation committee.

"Don Strachey here. We talked the other day about the Greg Stiver memorial scholarship fund?"

"Yeah. How you doing?"

"Just checking — did anybody else contact you about the fund? There seems to be some contact-list overlap."

"Yeah, somebody did. But I said I'd already talked to you."

"Do you remember who called?"

"Jim Jameson? Or John?"

"Right, right. We'll get this straightened out. Sorry to have troubled you."

"No problem."

I skipped Millicent Blessing at SUNY; she was probably still waiting for the BBC America crew to show up.

Melanie Fravel at HCCC answered her own phone.

"Hi, Ms. Fravel. It's agent Don Strachey. I was in your

office yesterday morning about the case involving misuse of assemblymen's names?"

"Oh, sure. How are you today, Mr. Strachey?"

"I'm well, thank you. And you?"

"I'm super. But I hate this cold weather in June."

"Well, that's the Northeast for you. But if you don't like the weather, wait a day and it'll change."

She chuckled. "What can I do for you?"

"We talked yesterday about duplication of effort among law enforcement agencies. You told me that a John Jameson had visited you previously about the same case I'm working on. I'm curious. Has he by chance been in contact with you since I came by yesterday?"

"Funny you should ask. Mr. Jameson hasn't, but another man was here yesterday afternoon only a couple of hours after you left. He was asking the same questions about the same situation, and he was asking about you. He seemed to know you."

"Hm. What was his name?"

"Robert Smith."

"That sounds phony to me."

"Well, that's what *I* thought. I have to say, I was suspicious. He said he worked for the federal government, but his badge didn't look anything like yours. And he just didn't inspire the same kind of trust that you do."

"Can you describe this man?"

"He could have been Mr. Jameson's cousin. Very sort of Slavic and quite big."

"Another Serb war criminal?"

She laughed. "Those are your words, not mine."

"But well turned out for a Balkan thug?"

"Well, yes. In a Paulie Walnuts sort of way."

"Sorry to have troubled you again. I'm going to get this

straightened out if it kills me."

"I hope you don't have to go that far, ha ha."

CHAPTER TWENTY-SIX

A mutual friend gave me the name of a lean and hungry able reporter at the *Times Union*. It wasn't time for any of that yet, but I knew it had to be soon. I was running out of ears, cars, etc.

I spent the afternoon checking back with people. Janie Insinger and Virgil Jackman were both in good shape, and the McCloskey campaign had pulled back their security for the time being. Neither objected to this; Insinger said Anthony had been doing a running mocking commentary on her relationship with Kevin, and she was "like, getting sick and tired of both of them."

Dunphy gave me the information on who my new paymaster would be: something called the Fund for Restoring Ethics in Journalism.

I said, "Is that a joke?"

He laughed. "Of course it is."

I made a number of calls in which I impersonated a Louderbush staffer — in for a dime, in for a dollar — and tried to find out if the assemblyman had intervened on behalf of other young male job seekers. "Hello, yes, I'm just following up on Assemblyman Kenyon Louderbush's endorsement of a faculty position applicant at your institution some years ago. The assemblyman wishes to know if everything worked out to the college's satisfaction…. The applicants name? I don't seem to have it here. Oh it was, uh…." I couldn't say it was that handsome young fellow with the cracked ribs, so nobody had a clue as to what I was talking about.

Then Giannopolous called. "I got hold of something you wanted. Louderbush's cell phone contacts over the past two weeks."

"Excellent."

"Most are just numbers, but some are voice mails. I've got it on a disk. Can somebody drop it off somewhere?"

I packed up my laptop, my weapon and my personal gear and drove out to Colonie, where I took a room at a Comfort Inn. Bud's cousin Ephram, who was even smaller and weirder looking than Bud, arrived ten minutes later with an envelope, the second of the day for me to open.

Some of the numbers Louderbush called or had been called from had names attached to them, and some didn't. The only name I recognized was Deidre. I figured I'd contact Bud and ask him to obtain a list of Louderbush's office staff so that I could probably eliminate them as persons of interest.

But that wasn't going to be necessary. I listened to a number of innocuous voice mail messages — meet for lunch, campaign meeting at four, don't forget Heather's birthday — before I landed on this one.

A male voice choked out, between sobs, "I didn't mean it, I didn't mean it, I didn't mean it! I have to see you, I have to see you, I have to see you!"

The name of the caller was Trey, and I noted his number. Louderbush had returned Trey's call on the same day, but there was no recording of what was said. The date of the call was June 19, the night Louderbush arranged to meet me at the Motel 6 but never showed.

I called Bud back, and within an hour I had Trey Bigelow's address in New Baltimore, fifteen miles down the Hudson from Albany.

§ § § §

I didn't know what Louderbush's car looked like, so I had no way of knowing if the twenty-year-old Ford Fiesta parked in the driveway of the house was his. It seemed unlikely that he would be visiting his boyfriend at five forty on a Tuesday afternoon. He was probably at the Capitol in Albany attending to important legislative business, like not passing the budget.

The house, on a side street uphill from the river, was a single-story 1920s stucco cottage that was not in the best of repair. An old trellis was leaning off the right wall, and nothing was growing up it. Any flowering bushes that had once graced the area around the cavelike front porch — hydrangea? forsythia? — had long since been cut back to the roots.

I pulled in behind the Ford and noted the Louderbush bumper sticker on the rear.

Bigelow didn't answer the door right away. But he finally opened it using the one arm he had that wasn't in a sling.

I said, "I don't know you at all, but whoever you are, you deserve better than Kenyon Louderbush."

He started to close the door, but I got a foot and a shoulder between the door and the jamb. "Either you talk to me or you talk to somebody who's going to be a lot less sympathetic and understanding than I am."

"Well, fuck, I can see I certainly deserve better than *you*."

Indicating the sling, I said, "Is this what you really want?"

I pushed my way on into the foyer and shut the door behind me.

He said, "Who are you, anyway? Are you, like, from the SPCA?" I could smell the beer on his breath.

"You know," I said, "this time it's your arm. The next time it could be your neck."

"He already did that. Collarbone anyways."

He was tall and gawky, with a beaky nose, a nice set of cheekbones and huge green eyes. His big head of flaxen hair needed tending to, and his jeans and tank top were stained with what could have been Chef Boyardee or could have been blood. The living room, through an archway to the left, was a mess — beer cans, supermarket tabloids, an empty pizza box — and the TV was tuned to Judge Judy.

I said, "What do you think the judge would have to say about the way Louderbush beats you?"

He said, "She'd throw his ass in jail," and then he began to tear up. "Hey, look, I have to get ready for work. I don't know who you are, but I can't talk to you. I gotta pull my shit together, man."

"Where do you work?"

"Price Chopper. Checkout."

"You're miserable. You're a mess. Don't you want out of this?"

"Yes. No. Yes and no. I mean, yes. Yes, I think I do. I've had e-fucking-nuff."

"It's not as if you're dependent on him."

"No, not financially. Though he helps me out. Beer money."

I pushed a pizza box aside and sat on the couch. Judge Judy was giving a tongue lashing to a black woman with impressive décolletage and a hairdo that looked like a small Las Vegas casino.

"What do you get out of it?"

"Unconditional love." He looked at me with the big eyes and more tears ran down his cheeks.

"What am I not understanding here? The conditions seem to be, he gets to seriously hurt you."

He perched on the edge of a folding metal chair. "It's usually not serious. This thing" — the arm — "is unusual. I don't think he meant to break it."

"What did you tell the hospital?"

"That I fell off a ladder."

"Do you have health insurance?"

"No, I'm not full-time. But Kenyon takes care of it. He has state insurance, and he gave me some fake card that says I'm one of his kids. He says I can say I'm adopted."

"How old are you, Trey?"

"Nineteen."

"Where did you meet Kenyon?"

"Online. Silver Daddies. He looked so butch and so sexy and so dangerous. That appealed to me. I'd been in this type of relationship before, but never with a dude who was so rough and important."

"And you really want to keep this up? It's only a matter of time before you suffer brain damage or something else that can't be fixed. Do you want to end up in a wheelchair at your age?"

"Maybe. I know I have low self-esteem. Maybe that's the only thing I'm good for. Being treated like shit."

"Have you ever tried to get out of the relationship?"

"A couple times. But it's just pretend. It's just so Kenyon can come down and get really liquored up and beat the crap out of me. He scares me though. One time I really meant it. He broke my fucking nose and it hurt like all get-out, and I told him that was *it*. I was serious this time, and he knew it. He went bananas. He was drunk as shit, and he started yelling about how if I tried to leave him he would kill me. He said he did it before — shoved some kid off a roof. Some SUNY student. I believed him too. He was so wild that night and crazy drunk."

"Did he mention the SUNY student's name?"

"I think it was one he mentioned before. Greg somebody. Kenyon had gotten this kid a job somewhere — Price Chopper maybe — and then the kid changed his mind about getting pounded by Kenyon all the time. He had some friends who talked him out of it. And when he told Kenyon he was breaking it off, Kenyon chased him up on a roof somewhere and pushed him off and killed him. He said every time I think about locking my door when he wants to come down here and get a little and then kick the crap out of me, I should remember what happened to this other poor kid."

"So you think it's true?"

"Sure. Kenyon's a celebrity. They can get away with shit like that."

"What if somebody offered to protect you from Kenyon? Get you into some kind of program?"

"Like Judge Judy?"

"I don't know about that."

"What about *The Price is Right*?"

"No, I meant some kind of program to help you deal with your need to get beaten up by your boyfriends."

"Like shrinks?"

"Sure, some kind of counseling. Have you ever been in a relationship with a man that was just pleasant and fun and nonviolent? Like friendship except with sex, too?"

"Yeah, in high school. With Jason Phipps. But my dad caught us one time and beat the holy bejesus out of me."

"I'm sure I can get you into something. And if you have no health insurance, I know some people who will help out on that end."

"So, what are you? Are you with the government? I'm not under arrest, am I?"

"No, I'm not connected with the government. I'm private."

"What happened to your ear?"

"Somebody hit me. But I was an unwilling victim. If I run into the guy again — and I hope to — I'll try to put him behind bars."

"In jail."

"You bet."

"So, let me get this straight. You're not one of Kenyon's other boyfriends?"

"No. There are others?"

"Two, I think. But I only know the name of one, Scott Hemmerer. I met him at a bar on Central Avenue one time. He had a big shiner, and I'd had a few, and I asked him if Kenyon Louderbush had socked him, and he just about fell off his chair."

"Do you know how I can get in touch with Scott? I'd like to talk to him."

"Yeah, he works at Dunkin' Donuts on Lark. But he's not

there now."

"How do you know that?"

"I heard he was in the hospital."

CHAPTER TWENTY-SEVEN

I phoned Bud and made arrangements for his cousin to pick up the recording of my conversation with Trey Bigelow and get it onto a couple of disks that would be stored in two separate locations.

I called Albany Med and learned that there was a Scott Hemmerer who was a patient in an orthopedic unit there, but I wasn't about to descend on him just yet.

Timmy called to check up on me, and I said, "I'm at the Comfort Inn in Colony. Would you mind coming out here for a few days? It's better if we stay away from the house, because I'm closing in on what's actually going on in this thing, and I have a bad feeling the Serbians are going to turn up again. And this time they're going to really mean business."

"Oh please. Worse than your car and your ear?"

"You know how the Balkans are."

"I'm having dinner with Myron and some big donor he's reeling in. I can get to the motel around nine. But how did everything change so fast? I thought Louderbush had brilliantly checkmated you and McCloskey."

I described my visit with Trey Bigelow and his list of grotesque revelations.

"Are you surprised?"

"No. After Stiver died — or Louderbush killed him — the only thing that really changed with this guy was, he switched MOs. Instead of seducing young academics, he began trolling online for down and out, low-IQ kids who were going to be even more malleable. He's got Bigelow now, and apparently there have been — and are — others. In one narrow but critical sense, it's Eliot Spitzer all over again. The compulsion, the hubris, the delusionary sense that he'll never get caught, and if he does he can somehow boogaloo his way out of it."

"But it doesn't sound as if Louderbush is going to end up with his own show on CNN."

"You never know. But this guy is not merely horny and hypocritical. He is deeply sick and deeply dangerous."

"He'd've made an interesting governor."

"Not gonna happen. I'm going to save the state of New York from Louderbush, and I'm going to save Louderbush from himself. Even in the unlikely event he ever got elected, he'd never last through the first year of his term. The guy is way, way out of control."

"He's not going to go gentle into the good night you have in mind for him, I'll bet."

"No, I'm counting on his staying in character, and I'll bet everything I've invested in this case that he will."

∫ ∫ ∫ ∫

I was having a beer and a burger down the road from the motel around seven when Bud reached me on my — his cousin's — cell and said, "I have some interesting tidbits for you. The cyberwars are heating up. Can I bring these shiny nuggets to wherever you are?"

He closed the door to my room behind him at seven thirty, and we both sat on the edge of the bed while Bud opened his laptop and showed me what a fellow hacker had sent him: some hacked files from yet another hacker who had once stolen the "incredible babe" girlfriend of hacker number two and now was going to be made to pay for his treachery.

I said, "I'm just glad all you cyberhackers are good Americans, and none of you are working for Muammar Qaddafi or the Syrians or anything."

"No, we're all patriots at heart. What we do is as American as Hostess Fruit Pie."

"So, these files are what? The e-mail correspondence between who and who?"

"Between my hacked hacker colleague — let's call him Todd,

since that's his name — who is known in the community for being totally bottom-line oriented — and a current client of his. Plus of course e-mails from his client to other parties which Todd made a point of hacking into and then saving for a rainy day. Todd is a man who is always available to the highest bidder, and on top of his amorality, he's good. One of the most talented in the field. His client this time is a name you may or may not know. His name is Sam, and right there is his e-mail address."

"Sam."

"Sam has regular correspondence with men in high places, as you'll see." Bud clicked and scrolled this way and that.

"Now here's a note to Sam from Stanley Weaver, CEO at BravuraCorp, the — what? — third largest bank in the United States?"

"Third or fourth."

"Quote: *If this nutcase Louderbush wins the Democratic primary, we are so so fucked. It'll be four years of McCloskey making life all but impossible for free enterprise to function. Can't you do anything for Merle? We'll help out naturally. Jay Goshen says you're working on something for him.*"

"There's a reply?"

More scrolling. "Quote: *Louderbush is a fag who beats up his boyfriends, and we're going to get this out. McCloskey has some clubfooted Albany PI working on it, and we're making sure his attention doesn't wander. This guy can't be bought, we've heard, but somebody who knows him told us how to keep him interested. i.e., push him around. I'm letting McCloskey's guy do the heavy lifting here, and then we'll sink McCloskey with some stories on how he's a dirty trickster unfit for office. Give me a week or two and Merle will be home free.*'"

"I'm trying to remember who Jay Goshen is. Is he the head of Herkimer House or Trevalian Brothers? I know it's one of the big brokerage firms."

"Trevalian."

"How many of these Sam-to-Wall-Street e-mails are there?"

"Forty or fifty. Some of the other names that crop up — at least as copies-to — are CEOs and CFOs at just about every major Wall Street bank and brokerage and law firm."

"Law firms. Well. I'm trying to zero in on which particular mischief Sam is creating here that's actually illegal. The campaign laws are so loose that candidates can get away with just about anything short of armed robbery. Even embarrassment doesn't count for a lot these days. The electorate is too cynical to care."

Bud raised a wait-a-minute finger and clicked and scrolled around some more.

"How familiar are you with the town of Hummerston, New Jersey?"

"I grew up in Jersey. But I've just barely heard of Hummerston."

"It's off Interstate 80 about thirty miles west of the G-W bridge. In recent years the town has built up a sizeable Serb community. Mostly people fed up with the racist, right-wing government in Serbia, but some, too, who are happy with the old Balkan ways of dealing with people with whom one disagrees. That is, rip their ears off, and so forth. Apparently these guys volunteered to help out the New Jersey state Republican organization, and Sam heard about them."

"Wow. Actual Serbians. Who'd have guessed?"

"You're lucky, Strachey. Those guys who went after you in the Outback parking lot didn't lop your ear off and make you eat it."

"No, they were under instructions to spur me on, not frighten me off. Somebody who knows me told Sam this is how I would respond to harassment. I wonder who. Any indication in any of this as to who that might have been?"

"No, but I'm still working on collecting voice mails. That particular morsel could be buried in there somewhere."

"So Sam hired these bad Serbians to rough me up? There are e-mails to that effect?"

"Just generalities. My guess is, Sam told them to do what they had to do to get the job done but what the limits were — this would have been done by phone — and then the e-mails were just to set the operation in motion and confirm that such-and-such had been carried out. You'll see the oblique and possibly coded language. A lot of it's in broken English, but some borders on literate. There's one guy who seems to use an alias, John Jameson."

"Do you have some other names and addresses in Hummerston?"

"I do. There's a night club called Belgrade Grotto. Liquor and coke — and dancing, both folk and pole. These fellows appear to own it. It's their Bada Bing club."

"I'd like to download all this and have it available to me as I continue to carry out my duties for the McCloskey campaign."

"I brought you four disks, each identical, with this material on each one. I've also included two CDs of your interview with the unfortunate Trey Bigelow."

"Thank you, Bud. There's lots of good reading here to keep me spellbound into the night."

He smiled at me with quiet satisfaction, his dark eyes bright with pride.

I said, "Most of what you do is against the law, isn't it?"

"Do you really want to get into that? Your own qualms and so forth? Okay. Sure. I'm a fucking archcriminal, no doubt about it."

"You don't worry about being prosecuted and being sent to prison?"

"Oh, yeah, I do. Prison sucks, I'm sure. But I pick and choose. I don't do military secrets, and I don't do Tom Cruise. I know what everybody else in the community is doing, and I stick with that. It's okay. Everybody does it is a weak moral argument, I know. But law enforcement goes along. Cops have better things to do, like terrorism and clubbing persons of the colored races for backtalk. Once in a while some doofus-y kid hacker fucks up a country's banking records or whatever. He's immediately clapped in irons, and I understand that. I don't want my bank statements arriving in my mailbox in Burmese any more than you do. But basically all a hacker has to do to remain at large is, don't do sabotage. I'll concede that political dirty tricks, so-called, can be a problematical area. But in this case I'm going to turn the raw material over to you, and it's going to be your set of practical and ethical quandaries from then on."

"How did you get into this line of work, Bud? Where did you study?"

"I went to Simon's Rock, but my gift for electronic information gathering may be genetic. I'm half Ethiopian and half Greek, and my Ethiopian mother was a spy for the anti-Mengistu coalition during the Marxist reign of terror after the monarchy was overthrown in 1973. She worked for the State Bank of Ethiopia, and she provided data on the regime's finances for the Tigreans and the Eritreans and for the CIA. My father's parents had a restaurant in Addis Ababa, but in those disastrous years nobody could afford to eat in it, so they got out and went to Greece.

"At some point in '81, Mom realized she was being watched and had probably been found out and was likely going to be arrested and shot. So my parents got out of bed one night and disguised themselves as peasants and commenced to walk to Khartoum, six hundred miles away. They nearly died from starvation and exposure and exhaustion, but they made it. My Uncle Getachew took the same route a month later. Thanks to a Baptist Church organization, they all ended up in Washington, where my parents now work for the Marriott Corporation. I was born in 1985 and my sister Yarukanesh two years later. She's quite respectable. Went to Brown and is a research scientist at the NIH. Don, what do you think? Am I unworthy of that amazing family history? Should I be embarrassed?"

"No, I think you just like living on the edge. You've found your own dangerous way of living among secrets."

He nodded. "I think you got me on that one."

"But aren't there less morally ambiguous ways of living this kind of life?"

"Like what?"

"I don't know. Cybersecurity?"

"What? For banks? For Wall Street greed pits?"

"What about antiterrorism? That's not so morally unclear."

"No, not usually. I could actually see myself doing that under the right circumstances. If antiterrorism meant more than just the police work end of it. Anyway, are you really the man to be lecturing me on questions of professional moral ambiguity? I know as much about the way you operate as you know about me, don't forget."

I thought about that. "I'm not sure what my excuse is. My mother only walked as far as Safeway. Generally of course she drove."

"There you go. You stand naked in your casual means-to-an-end-ism."

"God, Bud, you sound just like my boyfriend."

"Well, you were starting to sound just like my girlfriend."

"Then I'll stop. One more question, though, about these files. Is the Sam who is so busy behind the scenes orchestrating the election outcome for the Wall Street titans a man named Sam Krupa?"

"Yes, his name comes up in a couple of spots. My sense was that he was trying to keep his last name out of it. But some of the CEOs on a few occasions do refer to his full name. Who is that? The name sounds familiar."

"Years ago he was a political dirty trickster for Richard Nixon. More recently, he's believed by the political cognoscenti to be the man who — working for the same Wall Street gang trying to control the current gubernatorial election outcome — brought about the downfall of the bankers' archenemy, the crusading reformer Eliot Spitzer.

CHAPTER TWENTY-EIGHT

I left word on Timmy's voice mail that I would be out late. I said I'd leave a key card for my motel room at the front desk, and he should come on in and not wait up for me.

I drove over to Staples and bought four large padded envelopes. Then to Target for a cheap wash cloth. At *ampm*, I bought a bottle of Snapple iced tea, then went into the men's room and flushed the contents — way too sweet for me — down the toilet. When I topped off my rented Honda's tank, I also filled the Snapple jar with gasoline and capped it. Something was missing, so I went back inside and asked for some matches with the pack of Lucky Strikes I purchased, and then tossed the cigarettes in the trash and kept the matches.

The Honda came equipped with an excellent Garmin GPS. I had looked up the address online, and I keyed in the Belgrade Grotto in Hummerston, New Jersey. The driving time was given as three hours, ten minutes.

I left Colonie at nine and was actually in Hummerston by eleven forty-five — traffic was light — and I drove in and out of the parking lot of the Belgrade Grotto. A few cars were still there, although it looked as if closing time was probably going to be twelve. Among the vehicles was a black Lincoln Navigator with a green dump sticker on a rear side window. The club was a featureless single-story cinder block rectangle with a couple of blacked-out windows about seven feet up. Some grotto.

I picked up a coffee at an all-night 7-Eleven and then sat in the car and sipped it and read the Hummerston *Courier* from cover to cover. The health department had warned Mikey's Eats about reusing its cooking oil more often than the department recommended, and the Tarantella twins had just turned three.

Just after one, I drove back over to Belgrade Grotto. All the cars were gone and the place was quiet. There were a couple of security lights blazing out in front, but the rear of the building was dark. I parked down the road at a disused gas station that had been turned into a used car lot. The place was deserted, so there was no chance anybody would be making an offer on my rented Honda in the next ten minutes.

I made my way in the darkness behind a muffler dealer and a porn shop back to the Belgrade Grotto. A few cars drove by out on the highway, but none slowed down or stopped.

The Grotto had a mailbox next to the road. I flipped it open and inserted an envelope containing one of Bud's four disks. On the front of the envelope, I had written *From Sam Krupa. Copy to USCIS*, the immigration service. Handwriting? Fingerprints? I didn't think either was going to be a problem in this particular situation.

A car approached and I sank back behind a portable sign that said KARAOKE THURSDAY. After the car went by, I made my way to the rear of the Grotto. I assembled my petrol bomb — a bottle of gasoline with a gas-soaked rag as a wick — and then smashed a window just above my head with a steel bar that lay nearby. An alarm went off — *whoop, whoop, whoop, whoop!* I ignited the bomb and tossed it through the window, and it exploded with a frightful *ka-bang!*

I trotted back behind the porn and muffler shops to my car, tripping once but catching my balance, and got into the Honda and drove off.

By the time I hit the Garden State Parkway, I was no longer shaking, and after I got on the Thruway, with Albany a straight shot north, I stopped at a service area and left with a large bottle of cold water and a slice of pizza. The pizza smelled of gasoline, however, from my hands, and as I pulled back onto the highway I tossed it out the car window. Littering! That, I was ashamed of, and I almost went back and picked up my garbage. But the pizza was biodegradable, after all, and I was bone tired.

Timmy stirred but didn't awaken when I came in at four thirty-five. I showered and crawled into the second bed in the room. I lay awake for fifteen or more minutes, and then I was far away from it all.

§ § § §

Just after nine Wednesday morning, Timmy brought some coffee back to the room, and I woke up.

"Donald, I think I heard you when you came in. What time was it?"

"Late. After midnight."

"Where were you?"

"Making a mail delivery. Did you look at Bud's disk?" I had left a CD and a note for Timmy suggesting he examine the contents on my laptop.

"It's all incredible. Except it's not. They're the same people who brought Eliot Spitzer down. They're monstrous. They destroyed the US economy with their recklessness, and they're so morally bankrupt — or in such total denial — that they can't stand the idea of mending their greedy ways and abiding by regulations meant to protect ordinary investors and promote even a semblance of economic justice. And Sam Krupa, that evil old Republican troll! Wouldn't you just know."

"Everything old is new again. Not all of Nixon's thugs found Jesus and repented."

"So apparently you were being manipulated all along? Krupa wanted you to get the goods on Louderbush, so he had you roughed up, knowing how pigheaded you are and how you'd just keep at it?"

"The question is, how did he know me so well? Some PIs would have said the hell with this, these people must not be messed with. He was sure I'd react the way I did. There's a reference to someone who claims to know me and who assures Krupa I could be danced around like a marionette."

"I could have told them how you'd react to being pushed around. But I didn't."

"What do you think Myron told Dunphy about me?"

"Probably that you were stubborn and a pain in the ass but a decent human being and quite effective at what you do. And, yes, probably that you'd only be spurred on by a dangerous and challenging situation."

"I'd ask Dunphy, but he's obviously not going to admit to anything."

"I'm not sure he's that cynical. It could have been a lot of people. You're known around Albany."

I climbed out of bed and had a slug of the motel's watery coffee. "Did you listen to the CD and my interview with Trey Bigelow about Louderbush? Speaking of cynical."

"No, I fell asleep before I got to that."

"It's sickening. And heartbreaking." I described Louderbush's brutal treatment of this sad case of a young man and Bigelow's story about at least one other boyfriend Louderbush had apparently put in the hospital. "And then there's Greg Stiver. Louderbush got drunk and violent one time when Bigelow threatened to lock him out and said he'd once killed a recalcitrant boyfriend, and if Bigelow didn't cooperate he'd do it again. He said he had pushed this guy off a building."

Timmy sat down. "God. It's what the woman at SUNY almost saw happen."

"Possibly. Or it might only have happened in Louderbush's head. I'll have to ask him."

"Why would he admit anything to you? Anyway, he thinks he's got you defanged with all his blackmail crapola — the Bud stuff and so on that…who? Sam Krupa? — shoved through his mail slot."

"Yes, but I've got my own Bud crapola, and Assemblyman Louderbush's mail slot is about to be the recipient of another eye-opening deposit."

Timmy had called his office to say he'd be a little late, but now he was transitioning into his chief of staff mode, and he began climbing into his elegant costume. I said I wouldn't be back until late in the day and I'd be in touch. We kissed, and he was on his way.

I phoned the air service that had flown me to Kurtzburg and asked if somebody could fly me out there again that morning. They said they'd have to get an okay from the McCloskey campaign, but I told them I'd use a credit card and get reimbursed, and they said they thought Walt was around somewhere with his Cessna.

The day was breezy, and Walt did a couple of inadvertent loop-de-loops, but we arrived in Kurtzburg in one piece. There was no rental car waiting this time, but Walt suggested I call Dom's taxi.

I told Dom, "Special courier delivery for Assemblyman Kenyon Louderbush."

"Sure, I know where he lives. Everybody knows Kenyon. Good man. Make a good governor. No bullshit."

I got out the envelope on which I had written *Special Delivery to Kenyon Louderbush — from Don Strachey — Private and Confidential.* I walked up the front steps to the handsome old Louderbush house on Church Street and shoved it through the mail slot in the big oak front door.

Before I climbed back into Walt's little plane, I phoned Timmy. "Can you find out discreetly if Louderbush suddenly bolts out of his office later this afternoon and hightails it out to Kurtzburg?"

"Sure, I'll let you know."

Then I swooped back to Albany, checked out of the Comfort Inn, drove to our house on Crow Street, and waited for Sam Krupa to call.

Chapter Twenty-nine

"It looks like we need to talk," Krupa said. He spoke in a low rumble bordering on a croak that sounded about right for a man of his age — mid-eighties, I guessed.

"You bet."

"Can you get into the city?"

"Sure. What about the Serbians?"

"I'm not sure what you mean."

"Look, if this call is being recorded by either of us, neither of us is going to be able to make any use of it. We're at that stage, I think."

"The Serbians have been taken care of. They'll leave you alone. You know, you really didn't have to burn down their night club."

"I'm not sure what you mean."

"Now they're mad at me."

"Swell."

"I live on Sutton Place. Do you know the small park at the end of East Fifty-seventh overlooking the river?"

"I can find it."

"Tomorrow morning at eleven?"

"That works. And we'll both show up alone?"

"Oh sure."

I didn't give him my new cell number — I didn't want Todd monitoring my calls — but I gave him my e-mail address and said I'd check my Blackberry for any updates from him. Krupa recited his e-mail address, though of course I already had it — at this point, everybody knew everything about everybody else.

At my request, Trey Bigelow had given me the Albany Med

receipt from his last visit there. He'd also shown me the state employee's insurance card Louderbush had arranged for him to use, and I had made a note of the policy number. I called the *Times Union*, hit zero, and was put through to Vicki Jablonski, the investigative reporter I'd been told was the smartest and most aggressive in town.

"Don Strachey. I'm a private investigator. Rhonda Saltzman suggested I call. I've got a good story for you."

"Okay."

"I've got the goods on Kenyon Louderbush. The guy's not fit to hold public office."

"Uh-huh."

"Do you want to hear what he's guilty of?"

"Sure."

"Insurance fraud."

"All righty."

"Here's the thing. Louderbush arranged for an acquaintance with no health insurance to get onto his state employee family plan. This acquaintance is supposedly Louderbush's quote-unquote adopted child. But it's not true."

"It sounds as if you're saying Assemblyman Louderbush might be more of a humanitarian than some people give him credit for."

"Au contraire."

"Okay, au contraire."

"I'm not going to get into motives. You can if you want to. I'm just sticking to the facts."

"What's your evidence, Don?"

"Could I fax you a couple of things?"

"Sure." She gave me the number.

"They'll arrive in two minutes."

"Let me just ask you something. Are you by any chance

associated with the McCloskey campaign?"

"You bet. But that in no way alters the facts of the situation."

"Uh-huh. Send me what you've got, and maybe we'll go from there."

"What I can also tell you, Ms. Jablonski, is that there's a lot more to this story. It's going to finish off Louderbush's gubernatorial candidacy. Just follow the insurance card."

"What are you, some kind of Deep Throat wannabe? Exactly what are you trying to tell me, Don?"

"Just follow the health insurance."

I gave her my new cell number, rang off and faxed her Bigelow's receipt and the number of his insurance policy. Hospital records were confidential, but I assumed Jablonski had her sources, just as I did.

Timmy called at ten till four and said, "I called Louderbush's office and asked if he was available for a short budget committee meeting later today. I was told no, he'd been called back to Kurtzburg on some family matter, and he wouldn't be back in Albany until sometime tomorrow."

"Good. I'm headed back out there, then to the city. I'll be in the car a lot, but that's okay. I'll listen to some Mendelssohn and some Monk. It'll be good for my ear and for my soul to think about anything besides this disgusting case for several hours."

"Do you want me to come along? I'll be out of the office in an hour."

"No, I won't be back till tomorrow afternoon, so you might as well hold down the legislative fort and do everything you can to keep the state budget from getting passed for another day."

"I'll do my level best."

"But it's safe to go back to the house now. The Serbians are off the case. I talked to Sam Krupa."

"You actually *talked* with him? Was it like talking to Richard Nixon himself?"

"Krupa is less verbose than Nixon and, so far, less obscene. But we'll see how long that lasts. I'm meeting him tomorrow in New York, and he's not going to be happy with my proposal."

Timmy went back to work, and before I climbed into the rental car again, I phoned my friend at APD. I told him it would be a good idea to get out the files on the Greg Stiver suicide, because I thought the department would soon be reopening the case.

∫ ∫ ∫ ∫

"Where's your wife?" I asked Louderbush. "She might want to be recording this."

"My wife is at Pizza Hut with my daughter Heather's soccer team following their game, which is where I should be and where I would certainly prefer to be. I'll be talking things over with Deidre later this evening. Even though the packet you or one of your agents dropped off was addressed to me, she went ahead and opened it and examined its contents before I arrived home."

"I'll bet you're in Dutch now."

"In what?"

"You don't know that colloquialism? She gets the picture that your years of savagery are now known far and wide, and she's ripshit."

We were seated in Louderbush's district office, a room on the second floor of an old business block on Kurtzburg's Main Street. He was behind his desk, and I was in the constituent's chair facing him. There were the obligatory photos on the wall, framed and signed, with Louderbush and George Pataki, Louderbush and Pat Boone, Louderbush and Sarah Palin. On his desk was a framed family photographic group portrait, tinted.

"Yes, Deidre is going to need reassurance," he said. "Although surely this Krupa character isn't going public with this tired old gossip about me pre-Greg Stiver. It looks as though you've got enough on Krupa and the way he operates — like some scumbag Mafioso — to shut him up."

"I think so. Though the way we're headed here, it looks as though all three of the gubernatorial candidates are going to have to drop out of the race. Each of you has enough crud on the other two to force *everybody* out."

"Well," Louderbush said with a funny look, "everybody or nobody. Since no one of us can put his or her opposition research to use without being exposed as one thing or another by both other camps, in a sense we're all back to square one. And that's good. No one will be waging a campaign of personal destruction. The campaign can just be about the issues."

I sighed and said, "Well, in your case, Mr. Louderbush, it isn't as simple as that."

He saw it coming and reddened. "Not simple? How so?"

"I've met Trey Bigelow, and I know about Scott Hemmerer."

He had the humanity to look cornered. "I… I…"

"How many others have there been?"

He thought about that. "No others," he mouthed barely audibly with no conviction at all.

"And it gets worse," I said.

He waited.

"Insurance fraud. Bigelow's health insurance."

His liar's instincts kicked in. "Well, I'll have to look into that. I hope Trey didn't misunderstand something I said and come up with some fake insurance card or anything like that."

"He said you gave it to him."

"Oh no. That kid is so, so troubled. Troubled and treacherous, I now see."

"How about Hemmerer? I understand he's in the hospital with broken bones."

He slumped. "Bone. Just one. His ulna, I believe. Scott doesn't *look* all that fragile. He's actually kind of a rough little bugger. He and Trey must have concocted some insurance scam using my name and my state policy. You really have to wonder who's victimizing whom here, wouldn't you say?"

"Trey Bigelow told me that you got drunk one night and told him you had pushed Greg Stiver off the roof at SUNY. You were enraged because Greg told you he'd had enough of you and the beatings, and he was going to break off the relationship. You killed Greg, and you told Trey if he left you, you'd kill him, too."

Louderbush stood up. He shook his head. He sat down again with a thud. After a moment, he opened a desk drawer, and I pulled my Smith & Wesson out of the shoulder bag and raised it, barrel in the air. But what Louderbush lifted out of the drawer was not a weapon, just a bottle of Cutty Sark.

"I wasn't able to quit drinking, either," he muttered. He retrieved a plastic cup from a nearby shelf and poured himself a generous half cup. "Care for a shot, Donald?"

"No."

He had a healthy snort and then ruminated for a minute or so.

"You have no proof," he said finally. "Just the word of that fucked up little fairy."

"Of the murder, no, there's no smoking gun. But the insurance fraud is going to sink your political career. I've already passed that part of it to an investigative reporter. And she'll undoubtedly dredge up most of the rest — the young men, the beatings, the hypocrisy."

He smirked. "Oh, do you think I've been hypocritical? I've supported civil unions, hate crime laws, equal rights for gays in every case except gay marriage. The marriage thing is simply not politically tenable in this district. As far as I'm personally concerned, if homosexuals want to attempt to set up housekeeping and mate like real men and real women, that's up to them."

"You don't seem to include yourself in the category of homosexual."

"Of course I don't. Homosexuals are weak. Homosexuals are sick. Homosexuals are people who like to have their teeth kicked out. Do I look like one of those people? Could anybody possibly mistake me for such pathetic scum?"

He finished off the Cutty Sark in the cup and poured himself another half cup.

"As I understand it, Mr. Louderbush, you had sex with your male partners before you beat them. You seem actually to be of two minds about homosexuality."

"If any of these trash you've been talking to asserted that I myself have ever been anally penetrated, they are lying or delusional."

"No one went into particulars. I didn't ask. I didn't really want to know."

"So, leave me with just this one shred of self-respect, will you, please?"

He poured himself another drink, although this time he nearly missed the cup and splashed whiskey on some documents on his desk. He was getting as drunk as he could as fast as he could. Was he then going to kiss me? Punch me in the face?

I said, "I'm going to go after you on the Stiver death. There's a witness who saw two people on the Quad Four roof before Greg fell. And if you went into a drunken rage and admitted to Trey Bigelow that you shoved Greg over the edge, you might have admitted the same thing — bragged about it — to other men under similar circumstances. If so, I'm going to find these men and depose them and they are going to form a queue outside the Albany DA's office. You killed a decent, screwed up young gay man with his life ahead of him, and you're not going to get away with it."

Louderbush stood up and shook his head again over and over. He looked down at the family photo on his desk, and he began to snuffle. Suddenly he croaked out, "I'm sorry, Deidre, I'm so sorry!"

He sat down again with a *thunk* — seemed to collapse into his chair — but before I realized what he was up to, he was up again, fast, turned, and flung open a window behind him and dove into the cool evening air.

I raced out of the office and down the stairs to Main Street. Cars had stopped, and a few passers-by had already gathered to gawk and exclaim into their cell phones. Heaped on the sidewalk, Louderbush was breathing well enough, but he was still weeping, from physical and all kinds of other deeper pain. One arm was twisted weirdly, and one leg was ominously misshapen, too.

CHAPTER THIRTY

Just after two in the morning, I checked into a motel off the Thruway, near Kingston. I was spent, and I was still mad.

Louderbush had tried to tell the cops I'd pushed him out the window, but three teenagers down on the street had seen him dive out on his own. Also, the cops could smell the whiskey on his breath, and the hospital he was hauled off to would undoubtedly verify that the assemblyman had been inebriated when he fell or jumped from his office window. I told the police I had been interviewing Louderbush for an article in *Le Monde* when he began acting strangely and then plunged out the window. One cop said, "Some people can't hold their liquor."

I was back on the road by eight Thursday morning, and just after nine WCBS news radio reported that gubernatorial candidate Kenyon Louderbush was in an upstate hospital recovering from injuries suffered in a fall the night before. No details were yet available, WCBS said, but "unconfirmed reports" had the assemblyman tumbling from a second-story window.

In another hour I was creeping down FDR Drive in the all-day, all-night rush-hour traffic. I swung off the FDR at ten past ten and found a parking garage on 58th. I told the attendant I'd just be a few hours.

It was a perfectly lovely June morning in Manhattan. I arrived at the small leafy park at the end of well-appointed 57th Street early and sat on a bench enjoying the view over the East River and, beyond that, of ever up-and-coming Queens. I watched the traffic shoving itself across the waltzing tangle of girders of the 59th Street Bridge. Nearby, a couple of moms kept one eye on their Blackberries and another on their tots in the play area, and a woman with what might have been a small squash racket in her hair led around the park a dog that looked like a giraffe wearing a grass skirt.

Sam Krupa ambled in right on time and sat down next to me.

"You're the only person in the park seedy-looking enough to be a private detective. You're Strachey?"

"Yep, I am. And you're the only person in the park sneaky-looking enough to have worked for Nixon's political operation. You're Krupa."

"Sneaky-looking? Nobody except John Ehrlichman ever told me to my face that I looked the part. And that's when I was oh so much younger and oh so much meaner than I am now. I find it hard to believe that anybody would look at Sam Krupa today with Maalox stains on my tie and my cashmere Depends down below and consider me anything but a harmless old pisher, a fucking nobody."

"That's what I mean by sneaky. Mr. Krupa, you're still somebody. I mean, are you ever. Don't forget, I've seen the e-mails of your conversations with Stanley Weaver and Jay Goshen. And look at this ear of mine that's practically falling off. Hey, fella, you *did* that. You're…what? In your eighties? And when the masters of the universe want the body politic rearranged to their liking, who do they turn to? Sam Krupa. Maybe you pee in your pants nowadays — I'll take you at your word on that — but you still have the brass and the cojones and the cunning and the ruthlessness to get the filthiest of the filthy political jobs done. So, you aren't going to try to tell me you've mellowed now, are you?"

He had a surprisingly bland and inexpressive face, and the benign pale eyes gave away nothing. His epiglottis jumped around, though, even when he wasn't speaking, and it seem to be telegraphing something that might have been useful to understand for anybody knowledgeable enough to decode its machinations. I didn't know about his diapers, but otherwise he was dressed like a billion dollars, or at least like a client and probably social friend of a billion dollars, or ten.

He gargled out what might have been a chuckle. "No, I'm more worn out than I used to be, but I'm no mellower. I still like to kick the bad guys in the balls. Or the side of the head in your case. That's rare for me, though. Always has been, getting physical. I generally aim not for the solar plexus, but for the psyche, the emotional weak spot, the reputation."

"Like with Eliot Spitzer?"

He nodded, and the Adam's apple bobbed and weaved. "Oh, yeah, *those* stories."

"Somebody had to orchestrate his downfall."

A quizzical look. "Eliot didn't orchestrate it himself? That's how I understood it to happen."

"He didn't request sleazy PIs like me to follow him around and examine hotel linen with microscopes, and then tip off prosecutors and reporters. Somebody — a particular individual — arranged for those lurid aspects of Spitzer's spectacular ruination."

Krupa folded his pink hands over his beautifully tailored little belly. "Yeah, if only I still had the moxie for a move like that. Oh boy." He wasn't about to admit anything to some Albany pol's valet.

"This time it's not working," I said. "The Serbians were a bad mistake. You thought I was crude and you hired crude people to deal with me, and you got caught at it. And while you've got hacker Todd on your payroll, other people can play that game, too."

A tight smile. "I wrote the book on political hardball, and now other people have read it. Shouldn't I be collecting royalties?"

One of the moms had vacated her bench and led her little girl out onto Sutton Place. She was replaced by a middle-age black woman pushing a small white child in a stroller.

"Where," I asked, "did you get your information about me and how I could be expected to react to the rough stuff? A lot of people in Albany know that about me, I guess."

He seemed to take pleasure in looking me in the eye and telling me, "A PI here in the city who's much like yourself talked to people in Albany. I'm not sure who they were. But it did come back to me that Shy McCloskey knew what was going on, and he approved. He didn't want you wandering away or getting discouraged. Until, of course, he did. After you became more of a liability than a help, he had a couple of suggestions we gratefully accepted. Shy didn't want anybody to break your legs or what have you. Like a lot of liberals, he's a pacifist. But I'm told he said, why doesn't somebody just blow up Strachey's car? Then maybe you'd go away."

How much of this garish scenario was true? I supposed some of it was. Would I ever know for sure how it really happened? Possibly. Did it matter if I knew the truth? With the way things were about to go, not much.

I said, "I suppose you've heard about Louderbush."

"That you pushed him out a second-story window last night? I gave you more credit than that. I pegged you for a true professional who'd send him over Niagara Falls with a bag of bricks. Metaphorically speaking, of course."

"That's in the works. Louderbush is effectively out of the race."

"There'll be a withdrawal announcement later today, I'm told. Off to Betty Ford to deal with his alcoholism, sorry to disappoint his admirers, full support of his loving family — the whole bag of shtick. Not that you don't have other plans for him, which I'm sure you do."

"You bet."

"Bye-bye, Kenyon."

"And that leaves McCloskey and Ostwind to duke it out."

"That seems to be the case. Except, of course, you've got all manner of goddamned crap on us, and we've got all manner of goddamned crap on you. I'm assuming you're here to offer terms for a ceasefire. Am I right? We won't deploy our crap if you don't deploy yours."

"That's one of the possibilities, but it's not my plan A."

"*Your* plan A?" The epiglottis did a merry dance. "Shy McCloskey has entrusted his political future to some shit-ass

Albany PI with pizza stains on his jeans and one ear hanging off? I'm as amused as I am amazed."

"Why would you be? Merle Ostwind has apparently entrusted her political future and the immediate future of the Republican Party in New York State to a partisan hack from the Nixon era whose only goal is to protect the assets of a class of billionaires with the morals of a pack of hyenas. Or are you not actually here to speak for the Ostwind campaign?"

"Partisan hack? I take myself far more seriously than that. And you should, too, Mister PI Strachey."

"I'm aware of what the stakes are in all this."

"Oh, I don't think you do realize. Not at all. To you, it's just about issues or gay marriage or some other sideshow bunch of baloney. To me, it's about the power and the glory and the survival of the United States of America."

"Glorious banks. Glorious stockbrokers. Glorious hedge fund managers. Why do I have this nagging feeling that that's not what Jefferson and Madison had in mind?"

A dry chuckle. "Well, I can't argue with a sentimentalist. So, what is your Plan A, may I ask? Where *do* we go from here?"

"Mr. Krupa, here's the deal," I said. "What I'd *like* to propose — but I'm not going to — is this: both sides dump all the garbage they've got on the other side in reporters' laps — the newspapers would be ecstatic — and let the public make up its mind which political operation is the more revolting. Is it Shy and his seedy characters like myself and Bud Giannopoulis hacking people's phone calls and e-mails and impersonating federal agents? Or is it Todd and your Serbians and no doubt countless others doing the same type of electronic snooping, plus beating people up and blowing up cars in Albany residential neighborhoods?"

"Don't forget burning down night clubs in Hummerston."

"I still don't know what you mean by that. Anyway, I'd rather it all didn't play out that way. If this stuff got into the papers, the US attorney for the New York district might feel obliged to start empaneling grand juries. I think I could survive that, but I'm afraid Bud Giannopolous wouldn't. So, let's not do any of that. Enterprising reporters might dig up some of this anyway, but we don't have to make it easy for them."

"No, that particular scenario is out of the question from my perspective, also. Sweet Jesus."

"On the other hand, there is this: Our side is vulnerable, but yours is at far, far greater risk. Some of us might go to jail, but if the e-mails and phone conversations between you and Weaver and Goshen and the other bank and brokerage CEOs came to light — occupying pages and pages in the *Times* for days on end, a kind of Pentagon Papers of American capitalism — the consequences would be even more dire. It would create mayhem with markets, stock prices, bottom lines, bonuses. Jail would be a piece of cake in comparison to the damage the exposure of the Giannopolous papers would wreak on Wall Street. Do you know what I'm saying? Am I right?"

Krupa stared straight ahead for a long moment. Then he turned and peered at me. "You're in the wrong line of work."

"You mean because I was an English major at Rutgers?"

"On Wall Street, you could have gone far. You still could."

"No, I wouldn't last. Any more than I would working for Kim Jong Il. I'm too much of a pain in the ass."

"I'd say you're just exactly enough of a pain in the ass. Shit."

"So, what I'm proposing is this: Shy McCloskey stays in the race and Mrs. Ostwind drops out. She develops a case of the vapors or a hernia or something. The Republicans can then come up with another, presumably weaker candidate, and at least come out of all this with the markets secure and no major figures under indictment. Sure, McCloskey will win, and for four years he'll raise regulatory hell with Wall Street. But that'll pale next to what would have happened if the Giannopolous papers had ever gotten published and exposed the vast, appalling moral and social rot that you're promoting and that you represent."

Krupa gave me the fiercest stare I'd ever seen. Eventually he said, "You're insane."

I shrugged. "I don't think so."

CHAPTER THIRTY-ONE

"Holy shit, Strachey, I *heard* you were good, but this is incredible! You not only got rid of that disgusting degenerate Louderbush, but now Merle Ostwind will soon be gone, too. The New York electorate won't have to do much more than declare Shy governor by acclamation. I mean, yes, it was touch and go there for a while. But, man oh man, did you ever pull it out in the end! I can't begin to thank you enough. Have you ever thought of switching careers and going into politics? God, I'd be glad to help set you up."

"No, not politics. But recently I did briefly consider working on Wall Street. I'd join up just long enough to salt away a billion or two. Then retire to Thailand and live on spicy green papaya salad and invite the pool boys to hop up on my lap."

"Ha ha. Yeah, I can see *you* on Wall Street."

"With the pizza stains on my pants and my ear hanging off?"

"It'd be fun to watch from a distance, I'll say that."

Dunphy and I were in the private dining room at Da Vinci waiting for Shy McCloskey to show up. Dunphy had filled in McCloskey by phone, and the campaign director told me the senator was just thrilled, thrilled, thrilled with the way it was all turning out.

"I'm just glad," I said, "that I'm back in Senator McCloskey's good graces. For a while, his opinion of me was in the cellar, and that hurt. Did McCloskey mention to you, by the way, that it was he who was feeding somebody in Krupa's operation information about my psychic makeup so that my behavior could be manipulated? Spurred on or warned off, depending on the day of the week?"

The door opened and a waiter came in with an antipasti platter. Dunphy clammed up and waited.

After the waiter closed the door behind him, Dunphy said, "I don't believe that. Krupa told you that?"

"I know," I said, "that the guy is a major liar."

"And let us not neglect to add, major troublemaker."

"I just wondered if you'd heard anything about that."

"No."

"Okay."

"Look, Shy doesn't tell me everything. Like you, I just work here. But it doesn't sound like the Shy McCloskey I know."

"I'd hate to think that the next governor of New York was that cynical. I've also wondered at times, Tom, if you yourself weren't recording our conversations. There were times when you talked to me in language that seemed to be aimed over my head somewhere, perhaps at a grand jury. Was I just imaging that?"

He looked less hurt than bemused. "God, this is what we've all come to, what with the technology routinely available today. A bunch of paranoiacs."

"And it never occurred to Shy McCloskey to join the modern-day political throngs who spend so much time and energy on legally dubious electronic intel gathering?"

"Well, he's going to have to deal with the Legislature. So any dark skills he may have developed along the way would certainly come in handy. But tell me something, Don. How much does the *Times Union* know about what's going on with all this? A reporter named Vicki Jablonski called me today. She asked about you and your relationship with the campaign. I said you had worked for us in a consultant's capacity but that you were basically a volunteer at this point. Apparently you dropped the dime on Louderbush as to his putting his boyfriends on his family health insurance plan?"

"Jablonski doesn't know any of the rest of it, just the Louderbush insurance fraud. She'll dig up the beaten boyfriend stuff — maybe even the Greg Stiver death after I go to the Albany DA — and she'll think she's on top of the political story of the decade. I'm a little concerned that Louderbush himself will take the transcripts I gave him and turn them over to law enforcement, but since they incriminate him as much as anybody, that's unlikely. It's all a strategy of mutually assured destruction at this point. Nobody can afford to fire the first nuke because the retaliation will be instantaneous and massive."

"Wow. You could have been Secretary of State under…who? Johnson? Reagan?"

"Yet another missed career opportunity."

The door opened and Shy McCloskey shuffled in. He didn't look happy. He looked mad.

"Senator," Dunphy blurted, "should I send out for champagne now or…what's wrong? You look…pissed?"

"Shut up and sit down."

McCloskey dropped into a chair.

"I'm out of the race."

"What? No way. What?"

"I'll say it's my prostate. You can get something ready."

"But…but…."

"Merle called me."

"Mrs. Ostwind."

"Strachey, you have fucked this up *so* badly. Don't bother with champagne. And please don't eat any more of my prosciutto or provolone. You're fired, you fucking moron!"

My impulse was to start stuffing meat and cheese into my pockets. I hadn't been reimbursed for any of my expenses, including a charter flight to Kurtzburg and back, and suddenly this job was looking oh so much less lucrative than it had a day earlier.

"What happened?" I said.

"Merle didn't know about any of this. You did your little deal with Sam Krupa, and he called her today and told her she'd have to withdraw from the race, and she went bananas. She claims

— *claims* — she didn't know anything about Sam's operations: the e-mail and phone hacking, the Serbians, the rest of it. It is possible she didn't know. Plausible deniability and all that. Do what you have to do, and don't tell me. I don't like my people to operate that way, but some people do it. They think it keeps their virginity intact forever."

Dunphy said, "Jesus."

"So Merle says to me, she says, she doesn't give a flying fuck — not her words — about those Wall Street assholes. She says they should all be in jail. Merle is…what? The last Eisenhower Republican? She's nice. That's what Merle is, nice. Though if she was elected governor, the Wall Street people would run roughshod. She'd let them because Merle doesn't like to make waves. She hates a scene. It's rude. It's tasteless. It's not how people should comport themselves."

Dunphy was gazing at the prosciutto, and I wondered if he might pocket some, too.

"But the thing is," McCloskey went on, "Merle isn't dumb either. She heard what Krupa told her about the market taking a dive if all this hooey came out about the filthy secret campaign being waged on her behalf, and the Ostwinds no doubt have a portfolio of their own, as do their pals at the Mamaroneck Beach and Tennis Club. So she was able to grasp that she would have to leave the race to keep all this crap under wraps and the markets secure. Her only condition for dropping out was, that *I* drop out, too. Otherwise, she was staying in, and *fuck Wall Street* — again, not her words. So that's it. It's over. I'm going to have to go back and live among those half-wits in the Senate. My political life is finished, *finished*."

For a long moment, we all sat staring at nothing, each of us lost in his own thoughts.

It was Dunphy who finally spoke.

He said, "What about Andrew Cuomo? They say he's tired of being AG and eager to follow in his semi-beloved father's footsteps. And he'd be a terrific governor. I know *I'd* work to get him elected."

"Tom," McCloskey said, "I want you to stand up, walk through that door, and *get out of my sight!*"

Me, I wasn't even worth noticing anymore.

Timmy was able to wangle extra tickets to the Cuomo inaugural celebration, a modest event owing to the state budget crisis. Bud Giannopolous came along, and also his cousin Ephram.

Afterward, we all went down for dinner at Da Vinci. The place was packed with Democrats, all whooping it up and getting their political victory jollies. Tom Dunphy came over to our table and told us how ecstatic he was to finally be part of a winning gubernatorial campaign in New York State. When I introduced him to Bud, he turned pale, mumbled a terse greeting, and fled.

The papers that day were also full of news of Kenyon Louderbush's having been charged with assault by seven young men. One of them was Trey Bigelow. He had asked the DA if the presiding judge in the trial might be Judge Judy, but an assistant DA told Bigelow she was sorry that her office could make no promises in that regard.

Janie Insinger had the satisfaction of seeing Louderbush brought to justice without having to trouble her employer. She would not be called to testify. Virgil Jackman, on the other hand, was a major source for Vicki Jablonski in her extensive explosive reporting, and he was helpful to APD when it reopened the Greg Stiver suicide case. Of the eighteen young men who were discovered to have been beaten by Louderbush — only seven wished to press charges — three told prosecutors Louderbush had once gotten drunk and bragged about having thrown a college student off a high building and killed him. None of that could be proved, of course, but the multiple assault convictions would undoubtedly land Louderbush in Attica for what would be in effect a life term. It looked as if it would be justice OJ-style. Imperfect, but there you are.

Jennifer Stiver tried to get Shenango Life to reconsider its denial of her life insurance claim. But since a Louderbush murder conviction seemed unlikely, the company told her to take a hike.

She later told me that as disappointed as she was, at least she didn't have to turn on her TV and watch Shy McCloskey sworn in as governor.

The Tea Party, left in the lurch by Louderbush's exposure as a sadistic criminal, famously came up with a gubernatorial candidate — a rich, obnoxious real estate mogul from Buffalo — to run on the Republican instead of the Democratic ticket, but that turned out badly for them, too.

At the Da Vinci Democratic victory dinner, Timmy, ever the evangelical Jesuit I love, tried to talk Bud Giannopolous into going straight and avoiding ending up in the federal pen.

"Maybe," Timmy said, "you could do cybersecurity for some good outfit like Amnesty International or Human Rights Watch."

Plainly, this did not get Bud's blood coursing. He sat slumped in his chair and nodded glumly.

"Or, what about working for some revolutionary movement in the Middle East? There's an American political theorist named Gene Sharp whose ideas on nonviolent resistance in right-wing police states are being studied by young people in Tunisia and Egypt. I'm sure these people will need technical help with the social networks they'll use when the time comes to try to overthrow evil regimes like Ben Ali's and Mubarak's. That all sounds like a natural for you, Bud."

Bud sat up. He said he'd like to hear more.

About the Author

RICHARD STEVENSON is the pseudonym of Richard Lipez, author of thirteen books, including the Don Strachey private eye series. He also cowrote *Grand Scam* with Peter Stein, and contributed to *Crimes of the Scene: A Mystery Novel Guide for the International Traveler*. He is a mystery reviewer for *The Washington Post* and a former editorial writer for *The Berkshire Eagle*. Lipez's reporting, reviews, and fiction have appeared in *Newsday*, the *Boston Globe*, *The Progressive*, *The Atlantic Monthly*, *Harper's*, and many other publications. Four Don Strachey books have been filmed by here!TV. Lipez grew up in Pennsylvania, went to college there, and served in the Peace Corps in Ethiopia from 1962–64. He is married to sculptor Joe Wheaton and lives in Becket, Massachusetts.

The author acknowledges the trademark status and trademark owners of the following wordmarks mentioned in this work of fiction:

7-Eleven by 7-Eleven, Inc.

ACLU by American Civil Liberties Union

American Federation of Teachers by American Federation of Teachers, AFL-CIO

Bank of America by Bank of America Corporation

BBC America by British Broadcasting Corporation

Blackberry by Research In Motion Limited

Cadillac Escalade by General Motors LLC

Cinnabon by Cinnabon, Inc.

Cessna by Textron Innovations Inc.

Colgate by Colgate-Palmolive Company

Comfort Inn by Choice Hotels International, Inc.

CNBC by by CNBC, Inc.

CNN by Cable News Network, Inc.

Crowne Plaza by Six Continents Hotels, Inc.

Cutty Sark by Edrington Distillers Limited

Dasani by Coca-Cola Company

Denny's by DFO, LLC Limited Liability Company

Diebold by Diebold Incorporated

Facebook by Facebook Inc.

The Federalist Society by the Federalist Society for Law & Public Policy Studies

Fox Business by by Twentieth Century Fox Film Corporation

Fox News by Twentieth Century Fox Film Corporation

GE by General Electric Company

Good Housekeeping by Hearst Communications, Inc.

Hallmark Channel by Crown Media Holdings

Heinz by H.J. Heinz Company

The Home Depot by Homer TLC, Inc.

Honda by Honda Motor Co., Ltd.

Hyundai by Hyundai Corporation

KFC by KFC Corporation

Lincoln Navigator by the Ford Motor Company

Log Cabin Republicans by Log Cabin Republicans

Maalox by Aventis Pharmaceuticals Products Inc.

Motel 6 by Societe de Participations et D'Investissements de Motels

MSNBC by MSNBC

National Review by National Review Inc.

The New York Post by NYP Holdings, Inc.

New York Giants by New York Football Giants, Inc.

New York Yankees by New York Yankees Partnership

NPR by National Public Radio, Inc.

Outback Steakhouse by OS Asset, Inc.

Phi Beta Kappa by Phi Beta Kappa Society

Philadelphia Phillies by The Phillies

Poland Springs by Great Spring Waters of America Inc

Price Chopper by Golub Corporation

The Price is Right by Fremantlemedia Operations B.V.

Rutgers by Rutgers, The State University of New Jersey Instrumentality

Sam Adams by BBC Brands, LLC

Smith & Wesson by Smith & Wesson Corp.

SUNY by State University of New York

Super 8 by Cendant Finance Holding Company LLC

Time Warner by Time Warner Inc.

TCM by Turner Classic Movies LP, LLLP

Taser by TASER International, Inc.

Toyota by Toyota Jidosha Kabushiki Kaisha TA Toyota Motor Corporation

Triple A by the American Automobile Association, Inc.

Tylenol, by the Tylenol Company

UPS by United Parcel Service of America, Inc.

UVM by University of Vermont and State Agricultural College

Verizon by Verizon Trademark Services LLC

Walmart by Wal-Mart Stores, Inc.

WAMC Northeast Public Radio by WAMC Education Corporation

The Weather Channel by Weather Channel Inc.

THE DONALD STRACHEY MYSTERY SERIES

CPSIA information can be obtained at www.ICGtesting.com
Printed in the USA
LVOW131624190613

339337LV00001B/49/P